KU-792-637

PROTECTING HIS DEFIANT INNOCENT

PROTECTING HIS DEFIANT INNOCENT

BY

MICHELLE SMART

First published in Great Britain 2017
By Mills & Boon, an imprint of HarperCollins*Publishers*
1 London Bridge Street, London, SE1 9GF

Large Print edition 2017

ISBN: 978-0-263-07166-5

MIX
Paper from
responsible sources
FSC® C007454

This book is produced from independently certified FSC paper to ensure responsible forest management. For more information visit www.harpercollins.co.uk/green.

Printed and bound in Great Britain
by CPI Group (UK) Ltd, Croydon, CR0 4YY

This is for Nicky,
the best friend a girl could wish for. xxx

CHAPTER ONE

'ARE YOU WITH ME?' Francesca Pellegrini tightened her ponytail and glared at the two men sitting opposite her in the small draughty room of the family castle. 'Will we work together and build the hospital in Pieta's memory?'

Daniele threw his hands in the air. 'Do we have to discuss this now, in the middle of his wake?'

'I am talking about building an enduring legacy for our brother,' she reminded him crossly.

Francesca had known Daniele and Matteo would need a little convincing but had complete faith she would get their agreement. Hurricane Igor had decimated the Caribbean island of Caballeros only ten days ago. Twenty thousand people had died and the island had been left with only seven working hospitals for a population of eight million. Pieta, the eldest of the Pellegrini siblings, had seen the devastation on the news and had sprung straight into action in the way she had always so admired.

Despite running an international law firm, he'd always looked at practical ways to help those suffering at the hands of natural disasters, donating money, hosting fundraisers *and* getting his hands dirty. He'd been famed and honoured for his philanthropy and she'd been so proud to call herself his sister. She could hardly believe she would never see him again, his life cut short when his helicopter crashed in thick fog.

'I'm not asking you for the moon,' she continued, 'I'm asking you to put your skills into building the hospital Pieta was planning for a country that has lost everything and to do it in our brother's memory.' Daniele earned a fortune—he'd just taken delivery of a brand-new yacht!—but what good did he do with it? Who did her brother serve other than the god of money?

Francesca knew she was being unfair to the brother who'd always doted on her but what did it matter? Pieta was dead and the only thing she could focus on to endure the pain was continuing with his plan and thus continuing his legacy.

'I'm not saying it's a bad idea,' he snapped back. 'Just that we shouldn't be rushing into anything. There are security concerns for a start.'

'The country has been flattened. The only concerns are dysentery and cholera.'

'Don't be so naïve. It's one of the most dangerous and corrupt countries in the world and you want me to send my men to work there and for Matteo to send *his* staff there.'

Matteo Manaserro, their cousin, owned private medical clinics across the western world, performing vanity services for people who refused to age gracefully. He'd also launched a range of youth enhancing products that had made him world famous *and* as rich as Croesus. Francesca's mother was an enthusiastic wearer of the entire range and swore she'd only had a couple of nips and tucks since using them. Pieta had often said Matteo could have been one of the greatest and most eminent surgeons in the world but that he'd thrown it away in the pursuit of money, just like Daniele.

'I'm travelling to Caballeros tomorrow. I'll confirm myself that your security fears are unfounded,' she informed him without dropping her stare.

Daniele's face went the colour of puce. 'You are not.'

'I am. It's all arranged. Pieta had already earmarked the site to build the hospital on and put aside money for it and arranged meetings with government officials and…'

'You're not going. You don't have the authority for a start.'

'Yes, I do.' She played her trump card. 'Natasha's given me written authority to act as her representative as Pieta's next of kin.'

Her sister-in-law, who had sat in on the meeting like a mute ghost, looked vaguely startled to hear her name mentioned. Francesca knew she'd taken advantage of her fragile state of mind to get the authority but squashed her conscience. This was Pieta's legacy and she would do anything to achieve it. She *had* to.

Maybe if she finished what Pieta had started her guilt-ravaged dreams would stop.

I'm so sorry, Pieta. I didn't mean it. You were the best of us and I loved you. Forgive me, please.

'It's not safe!' Daniele slammed his hand so hard on the old oak table that even Matteo flinched.

But Francesca was beyond listening to reason. She knew it but could do nothing about it, like a child thrown into the deep end of a pool and needing to use its limited strength to swim to the shallows. That's how she felt; that she needed to reach the shallows to find forgiveness.

'Come with me and keep me safe if you're that concerned. That hospital will be built with or without you even if I have to build it myself.'

Daniele looked ready to explode. Maybe he would have done if Matteo hadn't sighed, raised his hand in the gesture of peace, leaned forward and said, 'You can count me in. I'll work with Daniele, if he agrees, on how the basic set-up should work, and when the construction's complete I'll personally come in and get it up and running, but only for a month and only because I loved Pieta.'

'Excellent.' If her cheeks had been able to curve upwards, Francesca would have smiled.

'But I agree with Daniele that security is a major concern. You're underestimating how dangerous Caballeros can be. I suggest we bring Felipe in.'

Daniele straightened like a poker. He looked at Matteo and nodded slowly. 'Yes. I can go with that. He'll be able to keep Francesca safe when she's ordering dictators around and protect any staff we hire for it.'

'Wait, wait, wait,' Francesca interjected. 'Who is this Felipe?'

'Felipe Lorenzi is a Spanish security expert. Pieta used his services many times.'

'I've never heard of him.' She supposed this wasn't very surprising. She'd only started her traineeship in Pieta's law firm a few months before, after graduating. Up until his death she'd never had any direct involvement in his private philanthropy.

'He's ex-Spanish Special Forces,' Matteo explained. 'He set up his own business providing security to businesses and individuals who need to travel to places most right minded people run away from and earned a fortune with it. Pieta thought very highly of him and I imagine he would have brought him in to act as security for this project if he'd...'

If he'd lived.

'Then we bring him in,' Francesca said after a pause she could see was painful for all of them. She would never admit it but the thought of travelling alone to Caballeros did scare her a little. She'd never travelled alone before. But she would be brave, just as Pieta had always been. 'But I don't need a babysitter.'

'You might have to wait a few days for him to organise his men,' Matteo said, 'but whoever he sends will be ex-special forces like himself and trained to handle any situation.'

'I can't wait,' she told them. 'I'm not being difficult but I have a meeting set up about the sale of the land tomorrow. If I cancel it, I don't know when they'll let me rearrange it for. We can't afford any delays.'

The whole project rested on her getting the sale of the land agreed. Without it there would be no hospital and no legacy. She *had* to get that land.

Daniele's eyes flashed on her. 'And you can't afford to take risks.'

'Pieta did,' she informed him defiantly. 'I can decide for myself what risks I'm willing to take and personally I think the risks are exaggerated.'

'You *what*...?'

The fight between them was diffused by Matteo raising another hand for peace. 'Francesca, we both understand how much you want to honour Pieta's memory—we all want to—but you need to understand we are only concerned for your safety. Felipe has a large network of men working for him, I'm sure it won't be a problem for him to put something in place for your arrival in Caballeros tomorrow.'

She caught the warning look he gave Daniele.

Daniele must have understood whatever the look meant for he nodded shrewdly before turning his attention back to her. 'You will do whatever they tell you. You are not to place yourself at unnecessary risk, is that understood?'

'Does this mean you're in?'

He sighed. 'Yes. I'm in. Can we return to the rest of our family now? Our mother needs us.'

Francesca nodded. The cramping in her chest loosened a little. She'd got everything she'd wanted from them and now she wanted to find her mother and hold her tight. 'To summarise, I'll take care of the legal side, Daniele takes care of the construction and Matteo takes care of the medical side. What about you, Natasha? Do you want to handle publicity for it?'

Although only married to Pieta for a year, they'd been engaged for six years and she'd thought her shy sister-in-law should have the chance be involved if she wanted. Publicity was important. Publicity brought donations and awareness.

Natasha shrugged her slim shoulders. 'I can do that,' she whispered.

'Then we are done.' Francesca got to her feet and rolled her shoulders, trying to ease the tension in them. Knowing she had Daniele and Matteo onside meant she could now, for one night only, mourn the brother she had loved.

From tomorrow, the hard work began.

Francesca clumped up the steps of the jet, shades on to keep the glare of the sun from her bleary eyes, to be greeted by the sombre flight crew. Her brother had been a man to inspire devotion and loyalty from his staff, and their obvious grief touched her.

If her heart didn't feel so heavy and her brain so tired from all the wine she'd drunk and the two hours of sleep she'd managed to snatch in the freezing room she'd always slept in when they'd stayed at the castle in her childhood, she would be excited to be on Pieta's personal jet. She'd never been in it before and it saddened her that now she would never travel in it with him.

The document Natasha had signed gave her carte blanche to do whatever was needed and use whatever resources were necessary from Pieta's foundation and personal estate for the project. She knew Daniele was angry with her for taking advantage of Natasha's fragile state and she did feel guilt for it but honestly, if she'd asked Natasha to sign over her house, car and bank account to her, she would have done so with the same glassy-eyed look. Before leaving the wake Francesca had pulled Matteo to one side and asked him to keep an eye on her. Matteo was more than just a cousin to them. He'd lived with them since he was thirteen and, being the same age as Pieta, had been his closest friend. Like the rest of the world, he'd been devoted to him. He would look out for Natasha.

Francesca was led into the main area of the jet, which was as luxurious as she'd imagined but before she had a chance to take it all in, she was startled to find a man sat on one of the plush leather chairs, a laptop open on the foldaway desk that covered what she could see were enormously long legs.

She stopped in her tracks.

Not expecting to be travelling with anyone, she glanced from the stewardess, who showed no surprise at his presence, back to the stranger before her.

The darkest brown eyes set in the most handsome face she had ever seen stared back.

Her breath caught in her throat.

It seemed as if an age passed before he spoke. 'You must be Francesca.'

The English was spoken with a heavy accent and from firm, generous lips that didn't even hint at a smile.

She blinked herself back to the present, realising she'd been staring at him. 'And you are?'

'Felipe Lorenzi.'

'*You're* Felipe?'

When Matteo and Daniele had spoken of the ex-special forces man she'd formed a mental image of a thuggish squat man with a shaven head and a body crammed with tattoos who wore nothing but grubby khaki trousers and black T-shirts.

This man was something else entirely. This man had a headful of thick hair that was darker even than his eyes and touched the collar of his crisp white shirt, which he wore with an immaculate and obviously expensive light grey suit with matching waistcoat and thin green checked tie.

He raised a brow. 'Were you expecting someone else?'

Unsettled for reasons she couldn't begin to decipher, Francesca took the seat opposite him, fighting her eyes' desire to stare and stare and stare some more.

'I wasn't expecting anyone.' She pulled the seat belt across her lap, doing her utmost to sound together and confident and unaffected by his presence. 'I was told I'd be meeting one of your men in Caballeros.'

Daniele and Matteo had made the arrangements, working their phones like a whirlwind throughout the wake to ensure there would be protection for her when she arrived on the island. She'd hadn't been told to expect company on her flight. If she had she'd have made an effort with her appearance, not thrown on the first clothes that had come to hand. She hadn't had time for a shower or even to moisturise her face.

The face that stared back didn't moisturise, she thought, feeling rather dizzy. This face was intensely, masculinely beautiful. But battle-hardened. This was a face that had seen sights the horrors of which were etched in the lines around his eyes and mouth, in the bump on the bridge of his strong nose and in the white flecks in the thick untamed beard that covered his jaw. This man had an aura of danger about him that sent thrills she couldn't understand racing through her bloodstream.

'Caballeros isn't stable. It isn't wise to go there without protection.' Especially not for a woman such as this, Felipe thought. He would have risen to shake her hand but her appearance had thrown him.

Both the Pellegrini brothers were handsome so it was to be expected that their younger sister would be good looking too. He hadn't expected her to be so truculently sexy, in tight ripped jeans, a billowing white blouse, and glittery thongs on her small, pretty feet.

'I didn't know it would be *you* personally,' she explained warily. 'I was under the impression you supplied the men to undertake the protection.'

'That is the case but there are times, such as this, when I undertake it myself.'

In the years he'd provided protection for Pieta on his philanthropic missions he'd got to know the man well. Throughout his career Felipe had dealt with death and loss many times; had almost become inured to it. The shock of Pieta's death had hit him harder than he would have expected. He'd been an exceptional man, intelligent and for all his daring, naturally cautious. He'd known how to handle situations.

Felipe had been propped at a hotel bar in the Middle East drinking the malt whiskey Pieta had liked in his memory when both Daniele and Matteo had called to say Pieta's little sister was travelling to Caballeros, a country quickly descending into anarchy, first thing in the morning, and that nothing they said would deter or delay her. He'd known immediately that he owed it to the great man to protect his sister himself and had set into action. Within ten hours he was in Pisa, showered, changed and sat on Pieta's jet. The only thing he hadn't had time for was a shave.

Francesca removed her shades and folded them into her handbag. When she looked at him, he experienced another, more powerful jolt.

Her height was the only thing average about her. Everything else about her was extraordinary, from the sheet of glossy black hair that hung the length of her back to the wide, kissable lips and clear olive skin. The only flaw on her features were her eyes, which were so red raw and puffy it was hard to distinguish the light brown colour of her pupils.

She'd buried her brother only the day before.

He recalled Daniele's warning about her state of mind. This was a woman on the edge.

'I was very sorry to hear about Pieta's death,' he said quietly.

'Not sorry enough to attend his funeral,' she replied archly although there was the slightest tremor in her hoarse voice. Hoarse from crying, he suspected.

'Work comes first. He would have understood.' On his next visit to Europe he intended to visit Pieta's grave and lay a wreath for him.

'You were able to juggle your work commitments to be here now.'

'I did,' he agreed. He'd had to pull a senior member of his staff away from his holiday to take over the job he'd been overseeing to make it to Pisa on time for the flight. 'Caballeros is a dangerous place.'

'Just so we're clear, you work for *me*,' she said in the impeccable English all the Pellegrinis spoke. 'My sister-in-law has given me written authority to represent her as Pieta's next of kin on this project.'

Felipe contemplated her through narrowed eyes. There had been a definite challenge in that husky tone.

'How old are you?' At thirty-six he was a year older than Pieta, the eldest of the three Pellegrini siblings. He recalled Francesca once being referred to as the 'happy accident'.

'I'm twenty-three.' She raised her chin, daring him to make something of her youth.

'Almost an old woman,' he mocked. He hadn't realised she was *that* young and now he did know he was doubly glad he'd disrupted his schedule to be there as her protection. He would have guessed at mid-twenties. Sure, only a few years older than her actual age but those years were often the most formative of an adult's life. His had been. They'd been the best of his life, right until the hostage situation that had culminated in the loss of his best friend and a bullet in his leg that had seen him medically discharged from the job he loved at only twenty-six.

She glared at him. 'I might be young but I am not stupid. You don't need to patronise me.'

'Age isn't linked to intelligence,' he conceded. 'What countries have you travelled to?'

'I've been to many countries.'

'With your family on holiday?' Francesca's father, Fabio Pellegrini, had been a descendant of the old Italian royal family. The Pellegrinis had long eschewed their royal titles but still owned a sprawling Tuscan estate near Pisa and had immense wealth. Vanessa Pellegrini, the matriarch, also came from old money. None of Vanessa or Fabio's children had ever wanted for anything. When Felipe compared it to his own humble upbringing the contrast couldn't be starker.

'Yes,' she said defiantly. 'I've visited most of Europe, the Americas and Australia. I would consider myself well-travelled.'

'And which of these many countries have been on a war footing?'

'Caballeros isn't on a war footing.'

'Not yet. In which of those countries was sanitation a problem?'

'I've got water-purifying tablets in my luggage.'

He hid a smile. She thought she had all the answers but didn't have a clue what she'd be walking into. 'That would make all the difference but you won't be needing them.'

'Why not?'

'Because you're not staying in Caballeros. I've booked you into a hotel in Aguadilla.' Aguadilla was a Spanish-Caribbean island relatively close to Caballeros but spared by the hurricane and as safe a country as there was in this dangerous world.

'You did what?'

'I cancelled the shack you'd been booked into in San Pedro,' he continued as if she hadn't spoken, referring to the Caballeron capital. 'We've a Cessna in place to fly you between the islands for all your meetings.'

Her cheeks flushed with angry colour. 'You had no right to do that. That *shack* was where Pieta was going to stay.'

'And he would have hired my firm for protection. He wasn't a fool. You're a vulnerable woman…'

'I am not.'

'Look at yourself through Caballeron eyes. You're young, rich and beautiful and, like it or not, you're a woman…'

'I'm not rich!'

'Your family is rich. Caballeros is the sixth most dangerous country in the world. Things were bad enough when the people had roofs over their heads. Now they have lost everything and they are angry. You will have a price on your head the second you set foot on their soil.'

'But I'm going to build them a hospital.'

'And many of them will be grateful. Like all the Caribbean islands it's full of wonderful, hospitable people but Caballeros has always had a dangerous underbelly and more military coups than any other country since it gained its independence from Spain. Guns and drugs are rife, the police and politicians are corrupt, and that was before Hurricane Igor destroyed their infrastructure and killed thousands of their population.'

It was a long time before Francesca spoke. In that time she stared at him with eyes that spat fire.

'I was already aware of the risks,' she said tremulously. 'It's why I agreed for your firm to be hired to protect me. Not babysit me. You had no right to change my arrangements. No right at all. I will pay you the full amount but I don't want your services any more. Take your things and get off the plane. I'm terminating our contract.'

He'd been told she would react like this. Both Daniele and Matteo had warned him of her fiery nature and fierce independent streak, which her grief for Pieta had compounded. That's why Daniele had taken the steps he had, to protect Francesca from herself.

'I'm sorry to tell you this but you're not in a position to fire me.' He gave a nonchalant shrug, followed by an even more nonchalant yawn. *Dios*, he was tired. He hadn't slept in two days and could do without the explosion he was certain was about to occur. 'Your sister-in-law has made an addendum to the authority she gave you. If at any time I report that you're not following my advice with regard to your safety, her authority is revoked and the project disbanded.'

CHAPTER TWO

THE SHOCK ON Francesca's face was priceless. 'Natasha did that? *Natasha*?'

'At Daniele's request. I understand he wanted her to cancel the authority altogether. This was their compromise.' As he spoke, the aeroplane hurtled down the runway and lifted into the air.

Now her features twisted into outrage. 'The dirty, underhanded…'

'Your brother and all your family are worried about you. They think you're too emotional and impulsive to get this done without falling into trouble. I am here to keep you out of trouble.' He leaned forward and spoke clearly. He needed her to understand that this wasn't a game and that he meant everything he said. 'I have no wish to be a tyrant but if you push me or behave rashly or take any risks I believe to be unnecessary, I will bring you straight back to Pisa.'

Her lips were pulled in so tightly all that showed was a thin white line. 'I want to see the addendum.'

'Of course.' He pulled it out of his inner jacket pocket. She leaned forward and snatched it from his outstretched hand.

The colour on her face darkened with each line read.

'That's a copy of the original,' he said in case she was thinking of ripping it into pieces.

She glared at him with malevolence. 'I spent five years working for my law degree. I know what a copy looks like.'

Then she took a deep inhalation before placing the document on her lap and clenching her hands into fists. 'Do not think you can push me around, Mr Lorenzi. I might be young but I'm not a child. This project means *everything* to me.'

'I appreciate that,' he replied calmly. 'If you act like the adult you claim to be there won't be any problems and the project will be safe.'

Her answering glare could have curdled milk.

Francesca was so angry she refused to make any further conversation. If Felipe was perturbed by her silence he didn't show it. He worked on his laptop for a couple of hours whilst eating a tower of sandwiches, then pressed the button on his seat that turned it into a pod bed.

Doing the same to her own seat, she tried to get some sleep too. She'd found only snatches since Pieta had died in the helicopter crash and that had been haunted sleep at best, waking with cold sweats and sobbing into her pillow. She didn't know which was the harder to endure, the guilt or the grief. Both sat like a hovering spectre ready to extend its scaly grip and pull her into darkness.

Had it really only been a week ago that her mother had called with the news that he'd been so cruelly taken from them?

For the first time since his death, tears didn't fill her eyes the second her head hit a pillow. She was too angry to cry.

She knew it was Daniele she should be angry with and not Felipe. Her brother was the one who'd gone behind her back and drawn up the addendum that effectively put Felipe in charge of her as if he were a teacher and she a student on a school trip. But Felipe, the hateful man, had signed it and made it clear he would enforce it.

It would be different if *she* were a man. He wouldn't be throwing his authority in her face and patronising her with her lack of worldliness if she were Daniele or Matteo. Her age and gender had always defined her within her family and it infuriated her to see it spread into the rest of her life.

She appreciated she'd been a surprise arrival, being born ten years after Daniele, twelve years after Pieta and their cousin Matteo, who had moved in with them when she was still a baby. The age difference was too stark not to be a factor in how they all treated her. To her father she'd been his princess, for her mother a female doll to dress in pretty clothes and fuss over. Daniele had fussed over her too, the big brother who'd brought her sweets, teased her, tormented her, taken her and her enamoured girlfriends for drives in his succession of new cars. She'd been his baby sister then and was still his baby sister now.

Only Pieta had treated her like a person in her own right and she'd adored him for it. He'd never treated her like a pet. His approval had meant the world to her and she'd followed his footsteps into a career in law like a puppy sniffing its master's heels.

How could she have reacted the way she had when she'd learned of his death? He deserved so much better than that.

She found her thoughts drifting back to the

man whose care she'd been put under. Who cared if he had a face that could make a heart melt and a physique that screamed sex appeal? One conversation had proved him to be an arrogant tyrant. Francesca had spent her life fighting to be taken seriously and she was damned if she would allow him or anyone else to have any power over her…

She sat up sharply. She would call Natasha and get her to cancel the addendum! Why hadn't she thought of this sooner?

Phone in hand, she put the call through. Just as she was convinced it would go to voicemail, Natasha answered it, sounding flat and groggy.

'Hi, Natasha, sorry to bother you but I need to speak to you about something.' As quietly as she could so as not to wake the sleeping figure in the pod opposite her, Francesca explained her fears.

'I'm sorry, Fran, but I promised Daniele I wouldn't let you talk me out of it,' she replied with sympathy. 'It's for your own safety.'

'But it'll be impossible for me to be effective if this man can veto all my decisions.'

'He can't veto anything.'

'He *can*. If he decides it isn't safe for me to be somewhere or to do something he can put a stop to everything. Your addendum gives him all the power.'

'It isn't that bad.'

'It *is*. He can call a halt to the whole project if I don't do exactly as he says!'

Natasha sighed. 'I'm sorry but I made a promise. Daniele is very concerned about your state of mind. We all are. Pieta's death…' Her voice faltered then lowered to a whisper. 'It's hit you hard. Felipe will keep you safe and stop you making any rash decisions while you're there. Please, try to understand. We're only doing what's best for you.'

If Francesca didn't know how fragile Natasha's own state of mind was she'd be tempted to shout down the phone that she was perfectly capable of deciding what was best for herself. But shouting would only prove that she was unstable when right now she needed to convince them all that she was perfectly sane and rational.

Daniele had brainwashed her sister-in-law. It was him she needed to speak to. If she could convince him the addendum was unnecessary then Natasha would agree to cancel it.

'Thanks anyway,' she whispered.

Her next call was to Daniele. She wasn't surprised when it went to voicemail. The rat would be avoiding her.

She left a short message in as sweet a tone as she could muster. 'Daniele, we need to talk. Call me back as soon as you get this.'

Proud that she hadn't sworn at him, she put her phone on the ledge by her pod bed. She had never failed to bend Daniele to her will before but this was a situation unlike any other. Cajoling him into buying her a dress for a ball—she was independent but not stupid—was one thing; persuading him to scrap a contract drawn up to keep her safe was a different matter.

'You won't get him to change his mind,' came the deep rumbling tone from the pod bed opposite, not sounding the slightest bit sleepy.

So the sneak had been awake all the time, listening to her conversations.

She threw the bedsheets off and got to her feet. 'I will. Just watch me.'

With no chance of getting any sleep she might as well have a shower and get herself ready for their arrival in the Caribbean.

Felipe ate eggs Benedict while waiting for Francesca to finish using the bathroom and adjacent dressing room. After nine hours on the plane he could do with another shower too. They'd be landing in Aguadilla in an hour, his Cessna at the ready to take them straight on to Caballeros and her meeting with the Governor.

He just hoped she was mentally prepared for what she would find there.

He understood her hostility. He'd never liked being subordinate to anyone either. Being in the forces had taught him obedience to orders but that had been a necessary part of any soldier's training. There was a chain of command and for anyone in that link to break it would see the whole chain collapse. He hadn't liked it but had seen the necessity of it and so had accepted it. Eventually he had climbed the chain so he had been the one giving the orders and now he commanded hundreds of men whose jobs took them all over the globe. Francesca would have to accept his authority in turn. Her safety was paramount. He wouldn't hesitate to pull her out if he thought it necessary.

Eventually she emerged from the dressing room.

'You look better,' he said, although it was an inadequate response to the difference from when she'd stepped onto the plane. Now she wore a tailored navy suit with tiny white lines racing the length of the jacket and tight trousers. Under the jacket was a black shirt and on her feet tan heels. Her lustrous black hair had been plaited and coiled into a bun at the nape of her neck. The effect managed to be professional and, he would guess, fashionable. It would certainly get her taken more seriously than the outfit she'd originally worn.

She answered with a tight smile and removed her laptop from the drawer a member of the cabin crew had put it in.

He got to his feet and stretched. 'I'm going to have a shower. Make sure you eat, we'll be landing in an hour.'

As he strolled past her he inhaled a fresh, delicate perfume and almost paused in his stride to inhale it again. Francesca smelled as good as she looked.

It didn't matter how good she smelt or how sexy she was, he reminded himself as he stripped off his suit, this was work where liaisons of anything but the professional kind were strictly forbidden. He had the clause written in all his employees' contracts for good reason. Their work was dangerous and needed a clear head. Any hint that the relationship between employee and client had crossed the line was grounds for instant dismissal.

Francesca could be Aphrodite herself and he would still keep his distance.

He switched the shower on and waited for the water to warm. And waited some more. Francesca had spent so long in it she'd used all the hot water.

He shook his head as he realised it had likely been deliberate.

'How was your shower?' she asked innocently when he returned to the cabin.

'Cold.'

Her lips twitched but she didn't look up from her laptop.

'After eight years in the forces where bathing of any kind was rare, any shower's a good one,' he said drily. 'But that's irrelevant to the job in hand so tell me what the game plan is.'

'You're not going to tell me what it is now you're in charge?' She didn't attempt to hide her bitterness.

'It's still your project. I'm in charge of your safety. If you're prepared to accept my authority with that, I'm happy to follow your lead.' He wanted this project to succeed as much as she did and knew the best way to stop her doing anything rash was to let her think she had some control. 'You have a meeting with the Governor of San Pedro in four hours. What are you hoping to achieve?'

Looking slightly mollified, she said, 'His agreement for the sale of the land that Pieta earmarked.'

'That's it?'

'The Governor is married to the Caballeron President's sister and given the job directly from the President himself. If he agrees there's no one left to object and I can start organising everything properly.'

'And if he refuses?'

She grimaced. 'I don't want to think about that.'

'You don't have a contingency plan?'

She closed the lid of her laptop. 'I'll think of something if it comes to it.'

'Why didn't Alberto come with you? He's got plenty of experience with this.' He watched her reaction closely. Alberto had been Pieta's right-hand man for his foundation. The pair had always travelled together, Alberto doing much of the legwork to get things moving. He knew his way around countries hit by natural disasters better than anyone and how to schmooze the people running them.

'He's taken leave,' she said with a shrug. 'You should have seen him at the funeral, he could barely stand. He's given me all the foundation's files but he's not capable of working right now.'

'Yet here you are, Pieta's sister, travelling to one of the most dangerous countries in the world only a day after you buried him, continuing his good work.'

Her jaw clenched and she closed her eyes, inhaling slowly. Then she nodded and met his gaze. The redness that had been such a feature of her eyes when she'd boarded the plane had gone, along with the puffiness surrounding them, but there was a bleakness in its place that was almost as hard to look at.

When she replied her voice was low but with an edge of steel. 'This project—doing it in Pieta's memory—is the only thing stopping me from falling apart.'

She had courage, he would give her that. He just hoped she had the strength to see the next five days through.

* * *

Francesca hardly had time to appreciate the beauty of Aguadilla before they stepped into the waiting Cessna. All she had time to note from the short car ride from Aguadilla International Airport to the significantly smaller airfield four miles away was the bluest sky she'd ever seen, the clearest sea and lots of greenery.

There were three men including the pilot waiting in the Cessna for them. Felipe shook hands with them all and threw their names at her while she nodded a greeting and tried to convince herself that the sick feeling in her belly wasn't fear that in twenty minutes they'd be landing in Caballeros.

'Are you okay?' Felipe asked once they were strapped in.

She jerked a nod. 'I'm good.'

'Is this your first visit to Caballeros?' the man who'd been introduced as James asked in a broad Australian accent.

She nodded again.

He grinned. 'Then I suggest you make the most of the beautiful Aguadillan scenery because where we're going is a dump.'

She gave a bark of laughter at the unexpected comment.

'Do these men all work for you?' she asked Felipe in an undertone when they were in the air.

'Yes. I've three more men posted around the governor's residence. All my employees are ex-special forces. James and Seb have both been posted here before. You couldn't be in better hands.'

'You managed all this in one night?' That was seriously impressive.

His dark brown eyes found hers. The strangest swooping sensation formed in her belly.

'While we're in Caballeros you're in my care and under my protection. I take that seriously.'

His words made her veins warm.

Francesca took a breath and turned away to stare out of the small window. When she put a hand to her neck she was further disconcerted to find her pulse beating strongly, and closed her eyes in an attempt to temper it.

During their last hour on Pieta's jet when she'd been working on her laptop, she hadn't been able to resist doing some research on Felipe's company. She supposed she should have done it before, when Daniele and Matteo had insisted Felipe's men be employed to protect her, but the thought hadn't occurred to her then.

What she'd learned had astounded her.

Matteo had said Felipe had earned a fortune from his business but she hadn't realised how vast his enterprise actually was. In one decade he'd built a company that spanned the globe, employing hundreds of ex-military personnel from dozens of nationalities. The company's assets were as startling, with jets of all shapes and sizes ready to be deployed at a moment's notice, and communications equipment reputed to be so effective the military from Europe to the US now purchased it for their own soldiers.

She could laugh to think of the macho meathead she'd imagined him to be. Felipe Lorenzi owned a business worth billions, and had the arrogance to prove it.

He'd struck up conversation with his colleagues who were seated in front of them. Their words went over her head. Her eyes drifted back to him.

He really was heavenly to look at. The more she looked, the more she wanted to look.

Coming from a wealthy family of her own,

she'd met and mixed with plenty of wealthy, handsome men in her time, but none like him, none who carried strength and danger like a second skin.

As he gave a low rumble of laughter at some wisecrack of James's—shocking in itself as she hadn't thought he *could* laugh—she found herself admiring the size of his biceps beneath the expensive fabric of his suit jacket.

Her gaze drifted lower, to the muscular thighs. They had to be at least twice the size of her own…

As if he could sense her attention on him, Felipe turned to look at her and in that moment, in that look, all the breath left her lungs and her mouth ran dry. Fresh heat flushed through her.

It was like being trapped. She couldn't tear her eyes away from the dark gaze before he gave a sharp blink and turned his focus back to his colleagues.

Francesca let out a slow, ragged breath and pressed her hand to her wildly beating heart.

Never mind being ruggedly handsome, Felipe Lorenzi was the sexiest man she'd ever laid eyes on.

What a shame he was also the most horrid.

* * *

Felipe had never thought he'd be pleased to land in Caballeros but as the Cessna touched down he sent a silent prayer of thanks.

He'd been busy chatting with James and Seb, the usual repartee, nothing important that couldn't be said in front of an outsider, when he'd suddenly become intensely aware *of* the outsider. It had happened so quickly it had taken him unawares, a thickening in his loins, an electricity over his skin, a lazy wonder of how her lips would feel beneath his, of what she would taste like…

Then, just as quickly, he'd pushed the awareness away and focussed his mind as he'd spent almost two decades doing, dispelling anything that wasn't central to the job at hand. An attraction to Francesca Pellegrini went straight into that category. Not central. Not even on the fringe. It couldn't be.

It was no big deal. He'd dealt with unwanted attraction before without any problems. It really was a case of just focussing the mind on what was important and the only thing of importance was her safety.

But there had been something in the look she'd

returned that made him think the attraction could be a two-way thing. He could handle it.

Francesca Pellegrini was off limits as a matter of course. Never mind his no-sex-with-the-clients stipulation with his employees—and if he were to enforce a rule then fair play meant he had to stick to those rules himself on the occasions he went out in the field—but she was grieving for her brother. He'd seen hardened men lose their minds with grief. *He'd* almost lost his mind with it once, the pain excruciating enough to know he never wanted to go through anything like it again. And he never would.

He'd spent his childhood effectively alone and where once he had yearned to escape the solitude, now he welcomed it. All his relationships, from the men he employed to the women he dated, were conducted at arm's length.

'Ready, boss?' Seb asked, his hand on the door.

Like much of the island, Caballeros' main airport had been badly damaged. Pellegrini money and Felipe's own greasing of the wheels had ensured a safe strip for them to land on. Looking over Francesca's shoulder to stare out of the window he could see for himself the extent of the damage. The terminal roof had been ripped off, windows shattered, piles of debris as far as the eye could see. Feet away from them lay a Boeing 737 on its side.

'Are you ready?' he asked Francesca quietly. She was staring frozenly out of the window, taking in the horror. 'We can always rearrange the meeting.'

She lifted her shoulders and tilted her neck. 'I'm not rearranging anything. Let's go.'

CHAPTER THREE

THE DRIVER OF the waiting car, another of Felipe's men, Francesca guessed, drove them carefully over roads thick with mud and so full of potholes she knew the damage had been pre-hurricane. Seb travelled with them, James staying in the Cessna with the pilot.

The Governor's residence was to the north of the island, far from the city he ran, an area relatively unscathed by the hurricane. To reach it, though, meant travelling through San Pedro, the island's capital, which along with the rest of the southern cities and towns had taken the brunt of the storm. She shivered to think this was the city she'd planned to stay in during her trip here.

They drove through towns that were only recognisable as such by the stacks of splintered wood and metal that had weeks before been the basis for people's homes. Tarpaulin and holey blankets were raised for shelter to replace them. People crowded everywhere, old and young, naked children, shoeless pregnant women, people with obvious injuries but only makeshift bandages covering their wounds. Most stared at the passing car with dazed eyes; some had the energy to try to approach it, a few threw things at them.

At the first bottle to hit their car, Francesca ducked into her seat.

'Don't worry,' Felipe said. 'It's bulletproof glass. Nothing can damage it.'

'Where's all the aid?' she asked in bewilderment. 'All the aid agencies that are supposed to be here?'

'They're concentrated to the south of the island. We just landed in the main airport and you saw the state of that. The other one is worse. They're having to bring the aid in by ship. The neighbouring islands have done their best to help but they're limited with what they can do as the hurricane struck so many of them too and the government isn't helping as it should. That airport should be cleared. There's much it should be doing but nothing's happening. It's a joke.'

By the time they arrived at the Governor's compound Francesca was more determined than ever to get the hospital built, not just for her brother's memory but for the poor people suffering from both the hurricane and its government's incompetence in clearing up after it. She felt she could burst with determination.

The Governor's residence was a sprawling white Spanish-style villa that made her hate him before she'd even laid eyes on him. There were armed guards everywhere protecting it, men who should be out on the streets clearing up the devastation.

As if reading her dark thoughts, Felipe stared at her until he had her attention.

His eyes were hard. 'Keep your personal feelings for the Governor to yourself. You must show him respect or he will kick you out and never admit you again.'

'How do I show respect to a man I already loathe?'

He shrugged. 'You're the one who wants to play the politician's role. Fake it. You've read Alberto's reports on Pieta's old projects. Think what your brother would do and do that. You're playing with the big boys now, Francesca. Or do I take you home?'

'No,' she rejected out of hand. 'I can do this.'

'You can fake respect?'

'I will do whatever is needed.'

Breathing deeply, Francesca got out of the car and walked up the long marble steps to the front door with Felipe at her side, leaving Seb and the driver in the car.

'Is there something wrong with your leg?' she asked, noticing a slight limp.

'Nothing serious,' he dismissed, his attention on their surroundings. She had a feeling nothing escaped his scrutiny.

After being frisked and scanned with metal detectors, they were led into a large white reception room filled with huge vases of white flowers and lined with marble statues, and told to wait.

The sofa in the reception room was so pristinely white that Francesca wiped the back of her skirt before sitting.

When they were alone, she said in an undertone, 'If this is the Governor's home I dread to think how pretentious the President's is.'

'Be careful.' Felipe leaned close to speak into her ear. 'There are cameras everywhere recording everything we do and say.'

She didn't know what unnerved her the most: knowing they were being spied on or Felipe's breath warm against her ear. She caught his scent, which was as warm as his breath, an expensive spicy smell that filled her mouth with moisture and had her sitting rigidly beside him to stop herself leaning into him so she could sniff him properly.

Clasping her hands together, she focussed on a painting of a gleaming yacht on the wall opposite.

She could not let her body's reactions to Felipe distract her from the job in hand. She'd spent her adult life rebuffing male advances. She'd turned down plenty of good-looking undergraduates at university, always with an appeasing smile and zero regret.

She hadn't wanted the distraction of a romance—not that romance itself played much of a part in a student's life—when she was determined to graduate with top honours. Sex and romance could wait until she was established in her career.

She sneaked a glance at the hands resting on the muscular lap beside hers. Like the rest of him they were big, the fingers long and calloused, the nails functionally short, nothing like the manicured digits the men at Pieta's law firm sported. Felipe was all man. You only had to look at him to know a woman's body was imprinted like a map in his memories.

A tall, lithe woman impeccably dressed in a white designer suit entered the room. The Governor was ready for them.

Pulling herself together, Francesca got to her feet, smoothed her jacket with hands that had suddenly gone clammy and picked up her laptop bag.

Her heart beat frantically, excitement and nerves fighting in her belly.

She could do this. She *would* do this. She would get the Governor's agreement for the sale of the land. She would make Pieta proud and, in doing so, obtain his forgiveness.

Felipe felt undressed without his gun, which he'd left in the car with Seb. He didn't expect any trouble in the Governor's own home but could see the bulges in the suits of the guards who lined the walls of the ostentatious dining room they were taken to.

The Governor himself sat at the dining table alone, eating an orange that had been cut into segments for him. The tall woman who'd brought them in arranged herself a foot behind him.

He didn't rise for his guests but gestured for them to sit.

Felipe hadn't expected to like the man but neither had he expected the instant dislike that flashed through him.

'My condolences about your brother,' the Governor said in Spanish, addressing Francesca's breasts. 'I hear he was a great man.'

From the panicked look Francesca shot at him, Felipe guessed she didn't speak his native tongue. Without missing a beat, he made the translation.

'Thank you,' she replied, smiling at the Governor as if having a lecherous sixty-year-old ogle her whilst speaking of her dead brother was perfectly acceptable. 'Do you speak Italian or English?'

'No,' he replied in English, before switching back to Spanish to address Felipe. 'You are her bodyguard?'

'I'm here as Miss Pellegrini's translator and advisor,' he answered smoothly, avoiding giving a direct lie.

The Governor put a large segment of orange in his mouth. 'I understand she wants to build a hospital in my city.'

Felipe smothered his distaste at being spoken to by someone chewing food. 'She does, yes. I believe her brother had already been in contact with your office about the land it could be built on.'

He sensed Francesca's agitation at being cut out of her own meeting. She had the air of a pet straining at its leash. He shot her a warning look. *Calm down.*

Another segment went into the wide mouth, the gaze fixing back on Francesca's breasts as if he were trying to see through the respectable clothing she wore. From the gleam in his beady eyes he was mentally undressing her. From the angry colour staining her face she knew it too but the quick look she threw at him told him to say nothing.

'Two hundred thousand dollars.'

'Is that for the land?'

The mouth still full of orange smiled. 'That is for me. The land itself is another two hundred thousand. All in cash.'

Felipe stared hard at Francesca as he made the translation, sending another warning to her with his eyes. He would have spoken his warnings but was damn sure the Governor spoke perfect English.

To his incredulity she agreed without a second's thought or consideration.

'Done.'

'The hospital is to have my name.'

Here she hesitated. Felipe knew why—she wanted to name it after her brother.

The Governor saw the hesitation. 'Either it has my name or permission is denied.'

Felipe translated again, adopting a harder edge to his voice in the vain hope she would pick up on it, slow down and negotiate properly.

But she was too keen to get the agreement made to see the danger she was walking into.

'Tell the Governor we will be honoured to name it after him,' she said in a tone so grateful Felipe braced himself for the Governor to pick up on it and demand even more from her.

A full mouth of pristine white teeth beamed. 'Then it is a deal. I am having a party here next Saturday.' That was a full week away. 'Bring her to it. I'll have the documents ready for you. Tell her to bring the cash.' He snapped his fingers and the tall woman stepped forward. 'Escort my guests back to their car. They're leaving.'

As they stood, Francesca, full of smiles, said, 'Please give my thanks to the Governor for his co-operation.'

She virtually skipped with joy out of the villa.

Only when they were safely in the back of the car and out of the compound did Felipe turn on her.

'What are you playing at?' he demanded. 'Where was the negotiation? And what were you thinking agreeing to pay a bribe?'

The smile on her face fell. 'What's it to you?'

'You've agreed to pay a cash bribe. You've agreed to bring in four hundred thousand dollars into the Caribbean's poorest country. Can't you see what's wrong with that? Can't you see the danger?'

'I've done what needed to be done,' she said defiantly. 'Thank you for making the translations, but you're being paid to protect me and advise on my security. If I want your input with anything else, I'll let you know.'

This was exactly what Daniele and Matteo had warned him about. Francesca was so determined to get the hospital built in Pieta's memory that she was a danger to herself.

Francesca didn't understand why Felipe was being so negative. The meeting had gone a hundred times better than she'd expected. She'd expected to be drilled for hours about the hospital itself, its capabilities and the number of people they hoped to be able to treat. She'd made sure to have all the relevant figures and documents ready for him but in the end it had boiled down to one simple thing: money. And Pieta's philanthropic foundation had plenty of it.

Felipe was taking his job as protector too far.

'What about your career?' he ground out. 'Did you think about that? Do you want it ruined before it's even started?'

Excited that they were heading straight to the site the hospital would be built on, his words took a moment to sink in. 'What are you talking about?'

'If word gets out that you paid a bribe to the Governor of San Pedro your career will be over. Lawyers are supposed to be on the side of the law.'

Dear God, that hadn't even occurred to her.

She swayed in her seat as hot dizziness poured into her head. For one dreadful moment she really thought she was going to faint.

In her eagerness to get the site signed over to the foundation, it hadn't crossed her mind that she could be jeopardising her career by paying the Governor's bribe.

'Pieta paid bribes,' she said, more to herself and for her own mitigation.

'No, your brother was always smart enough *not* to pay them and not as openly as you're doing and not verbally with secret cameras recording every word said. He would never have put himself or his foundation in such jeopardy. He acted with discretion and had other people pay any bribe through intermediaries. You should know that.'

'I would if anyone had ever told me. It wasn't in any of the files.' But it wouldn't have been, she realised, her blood running colder still. Alberto had told her to prepare to 'grease the wheels' with the Governor but Alberto had been half crazed with grief and there had been nothing written down and for good reason; who would be stupid enough to leave a paper trail advertising law-breaking, even if for good reasons and intentions? 'Why didn't *you* tell me seeing as you know so much?'

She'd been so proud and relieved to have got the Governor's agreement that she'd been oblivious to anything else.

'I assumed you did know. I could hardly tell you in the middle of the meeting—'

'We're being followed.' It was Seb's voice that cut through their angry exchange.

Felipe turned to look out of the back window. 'Black Mondeo.'

'I see it.'

Felipe's left hand gripped Francesca's shoulder, preventing her from turning to look too.

'Keep down,' he said tautly.

'But…'

A silver gun appeared in his right hand.

'What do you need *that* for?' she virtually screeched.

'Someone's following us.'

'How do you know that?' she asked, her eyes on his gun. 'They might just be travelling the same route as us.'

His eyes were hard. 'It's my job to know and if I don't know then I don't take risks. Now hold on.'

The hand that had been holding her shoulder moved so his arm covered her chest like an additional seat belt. A second later she learned why when Seb put his foot down.

She only just held back a scream when she found them suddenly hurtling along the bumpy roads. Caballeros passed by in a blur, the roads narrowing and deteriorating the further south they travelled.

When they missed hitting an oncoming truck by inches, she squeezed her eyes shut and clung to Felipe's arm and didn't let go until with a squeal of brakes the car came to a stop.

'You can look now, we're at the airport,' Felipe said, his voice tight. 'We've lost them.'

She let go and was pleased to see him wince as he shook the arm she'd been holding with the grip of a boa constrictor. The gun was still nestled comfortably in his right hand.

'On what planet is travelling at a hundred miles an hour over potholed narrow roads keeping me safe?' she demanded, all the contained fear spewing out in one swoop. 'We could have been killed!'

Her door opened and James stood there, a big grin on his face. 'That looked like some ride.'

'Your colleague's a maniac.'

'Who? Seb? Don't worry about him, he's done an advanced motoring course.'

'Shut up, James,' Felipe bit out, then to Francesca said, 'I'm sorry if we scared you but I did warn you of the dangers.'

'You warned me of kidnap and robbery. You

said nothing about a car ride turning into the rollercoaster ride from hell. You said nothing about being *armed*.'

'Would you have preferred we let them catch us? Should I have asked them nicely why they were following us and what they wanted? Should I arm myself with a feather duster to protect you?'

'Well…no…'

'Then let's get in the plane before they find us and tell us in person what they want.'

'We're supposed to be going to the hospital site.'

'That can wait.'

'But…'

The look on his face stopped her arguing further. It was a look that spoke plainly. If she didn't get out of the car and onto the plane *right now* he would carry her to it.

The adrenaline racing through her peaked to imagine what it would be like carried in his arms…

Humiliating, that's what it would be, carted off like a recalcitrant child.

Jutting her chin in the air, she twisted round and got out, snubbing James's offered hand.

'I don't know why you're ignoring me, I wasn't in the car,' he complained.

She couldn't help but smile weakly at his boyish charm even though he too had a gun in his hand. 'Shut up, James.'

'Yes, shut up, James,' Felipe muttered as he followed her, scrutinising their surroundings, his hand on her back, ready to throw himself on her should anything happen.

His heart still pounded from the adrenaline surge of the race back to the airport and he was as angry about that as he was about Francesca's idiocy. Adrenaline was part of the job—for most of them it *was* the job—but not like that.

Only when they were airborne did he put the gun back in his inside jacket pocket.

He'd seen Francesca's fear when he'd produced it.

Good.

Fear could be a useful tool provided one knew how to control it. She had controlled her fear well enough, he admitted grudgingly, but she had to learn her safety wasn't a game. There would be no compromises in that regard.

He closed his eyes and breathed welcome oxygen into his lungs.

He hadn't experience a charge like that since the hostage situation a decade ago that had ended in such destruction and his own medical discharge from the forces.

When they landed back in the safety of Aguadilla, Francesca found she could breathe again. Caballeros had frightened her more than she wanted to admit. The guns Felipe and his men carried frightened her too; a physical reminder of the danger Daniele and Matteo had been so keen to ram into her but which she had naively thought they were exaggerating.

Felipe took the wheel, taking them through rural byways where coconut sellers lined the road and men sat at tables playing board games. One minute they were driving through what looked like jungle, the next in the open air with the Caribbean Sea gleaming before them, then back into the jungle. Twenty minutes after they left the airport, they pulled up outside a pretty single-storey lodge.

'This looks nice,' she said, attempting a conciliatory tone at the rigid figure driving the car who hadn't exchanged a word with anyone since they'd left the airport.

Now that her adrenaline had settled she could appreciate that a combination of her fear and the awful realisation that she'd screwed up had made her come across as a spoilt brat. Felipe and Seb had done nothing more in the car than they were being paid for—keeping her safe. And Felipe *had* tried to warn her in the meeting, she remembered. But they'd been non-verbal warnings she'd ignored in her determination to seal the deal.

She would have to apologise.

'This is where we're slumming it,' James said, his eyes twinkling.

'Hardly slumming it,' she protested. 'It's charming.'

'Nah, not you. Seb and I have to slum it while you and grumpy here get to live it up in a seven-star paradise up the road. Don't party too hard.'

Both men slammed the doors behind them, leaving her in the back alone with Felipe up front.

He switched the engine back on.

'Hold on, I'll come and sit up front with you,' she said, but found the door wouldn't open. 'Have you turned the child lock on?'

He turned the car round, saying, 'Put your seat belt back on, we'll be there in a few minutes.'

She slumped back and folded her arms, her

warmed feelings towards him disappearing in an instant at his arrogant highhandedness.

'"Put your seat belt back on,"' she mimicked under her breath. *'"Don't do this, don't do that, just do exactly as I say."'*

He could forget an apology.

Not even the long private driveway dotted with security guards that opened up to reveal their perfectly named Eden Hotel could lift her mood, or the thought of calling Daniele with the good news. When the contracts were signed a week from now he'd fly over and check the site and get the architectural plans, which he'd promised to get started on, finalised.

But she would have to tell him too about her foolishness. He would be rightly furious with her. She was furious with herself.

She followed Felipe out of the car and into the sweet air, and hurried to follow him into the hotel.

And what a hotel it was. Francesca had stayed in many luxury resorts with her family while growing up but nowhere that could compare to this. The Eden Hotel was like a tall, sprawling villa set back from its own private sandy cove, its pristine white fascia covered in all manner of colourful climbing flowers and vines.

It oozed money, a feeling compounded when she stepped into a giant oval atrium with a waterfall as a centrepiece that managed to be both bustling with life yet utterly serene, evoking the sense of calm she so desperately needed. It made the Governor's residence seem like a trifling town hall.

Felipe strolled to the horseshoe-shaped reception desk and used the time spent checking in getting a handle on the turbulence still coursing through him. All he wanted was to get into the privacy of his suite before he said or did something he regretted.

Once they'd been given their respective keys he said, without looking at the woman who'd caused all the turbulence, 'Your luggage has been taken to your suite. I'll meet you in here after breakfast on Monday…'

'*Monday*?'

'None of the officials you want to see will be available tomorrow. Not on a Sunday.'

'But Caballeros is in a state of emergency!'

'Have you made any appointments?'

'Not yet,' she admitted reluctantly. 'I didn't want to get ahead of myself before I got the Governor's agreement. I'm planning to call everyone on my list when I get to my room.'

'They won't see you tomorrow. For all its faults Caballeros is a religious country and Sunday is considered a day of rest so we will meet on Monday.'

'If I can get appointments made for tomorrow then we go back tomorrow.'

'We go back on Monday.' He stared hard at her angry face. 'You can use tomorrow to do some proper research on what you're dealing with and be fully prepared.'

'Meaning?'

'The contract I signed was to provide you with protection for five days only. The Governor wants his bribe next Saturday, a week from now. If you want my agreement to stay the extra days then you need to stop acting like a brat, meaning you need to slow down and get your head straight before you make any more slip-ups. The deeds to the site aren't yours yet and the way I'm feeling right now I could call your brother and tell him his fears have come true and that you're a danger to yourself and should go home. *Buenas noches.*'

As he strode away, leaving her open-mouthed behind him, knowing perfectly well that only the threat of him calling her brother was stopping her from shouting at him and calling him all the names under the sun, he thought a day of rest would do him good too.

One day in Francesca Pellegrini's company and he was ready to punch walls.

CHAPTER FOUR

A PORTER SHOWED Francesca to her room, where her luggage was already waiting for her.

She'd assumed she'd be staying in one of the cheap rooms—if a hotel of this magnificence had anything that could be regarded as cheap—but found herself in a ground-floor suite so large, airy and luxurious she could only ogle in wonder.

She'd thought James had been joking about them staying in a seven-star hotel and while she was thrilled to be here in this sun-drenched paradise, she was worried enough to temporarily forget all the ways she'd been imagining inflicting pain on Felipe Lorenzi, the horrible, arrogant, patronising man.

She knew what a blunder she'd made but he acted as if she were the only person to have ever made one.

In one respect he was right. She did need to slow down and get her head straight.

Pulling her phone out of her bag, she called Daniele. This time he answered. He took the good news about the agreement for the site with muted enthusiasm. The only real animation from him came when she asked—nicely—if he would sack Felipe and get another security firm to take over her protection. He laughed. 'I told you that you wouldn't be able to wrap him around your little finger. He stays.' And then he disconnected the call before she could confess about the bribe.

She rubbed her eyes. Maybe it was best to leave it a couple of days before telling him. She didn't think she could handle any more rebukes that day. But Felipe was bound to tell him…

She could scream. What a mess she'd made of things.

Had she really? She'd gone to Caballeros to get the Governor's agreement and had achieved it. The hospital would be built. And she understood the foundation *had* paid bribes in the past. She just needed to speak to Alberto and discuss how it could be done without endangering the foundation. Or her career.

Knowing her emotions were too charged to think clearly enough to make any further calls, she selected a bottle of white wine from the fully stocked bar, poured herself a large glass and took it into the bathroom so she could have a long soak in the enormous jetted bath.

It was too late to change hotels now. She might as well enjoy it for tonight and see about getting them moved to a cheaper hotel in the morning.

But instead of relaxing like she so wanted, her mind refused to switch off. Everywhere she looked, from the gold taps to the marble flooring, increased her worry. This hotel was too much.

With a sigh, she got out and dried herself, dressed quickly and put a call through to reception.

'Can you tell me what room Felipe Lorenzi's staying in, please?' she asked. 'We're under the same booking but I can't remember his number.' She crossed her fingers as she gave the little fib.

When the number was relayed she gave a little start. 'Room fourteen?' she confirmed.

That was right next to hers.

Her heart hammering for no reason at all, Francesca decided to just go for it and slipped out of her room to knock on the one next door.

He answered on the second knock, opening the door a crack. 'Is there a problem?'

'Can I come in for a minute?' she asked, matching his frosty tone. All she could see of him was the shadow of his face.

He paused before answering. 'I'm about to take a shower.'

'I want to change hotels.'

'Why?'

'A hotel like this is expensive.'

'The cost of the hotel does not concern you.'

'It does. People work hard to raise funds for Pieta's foundation and give generously to it.'

'Do they give generously to pay bribes?'

'That's a necessity,' she protested. 'I know I went about it in the wrong way but you know as well as I that we wouldn't get permission to build the hospital without it. It isn't right to waste the funds on something as frivolous as a luxury hotel. Somewhere like where James and Seb are staying would be far more appropriate.'

The little of his face she could see darkened and when he replied it was in clipped tones. 'The foundation isn't paying.'

That alarmed her. 'Then who is? I can't afford it on my salary and I can't—'

'You're not paying either,' he cut in impatiently.

'Who *is* footing it?' It came to her in an instant. 'Daniele! He loves flashing his money and—'

'Was there anything else you wanted to discuss?' Felipe cut in again, not making any attempt to hide his irritation. 'Only I'm standing here without any clothes on and would like to take my shower, so if you don't mind...'

Francesca was unable to halt the mental image of him naked shooting like a spring lamb into her mind.

Oh, dear heavens...

He was naked.

'Was there anything else?' he repeated curtly.

He was naked.

'No.'

'Then I'll see you on Monday.'

Francesca stood before his closed door for a long time, her hand at her throat, her pulse beating like a hummingbird's wings beneath her fingers.

Felipe shaved his neck and trimmed his beard for the first time in three weeks.

It was guilt, he knew, that made his concentration waver enough for him to nick himself with the razor.

Guilt had been rising in him since he'd dismissed Francesca from the door of his suite.

He'd never had such problems with a client before and he'd had many clients and jobs that had been a hundred times harder to manage than Francesca and this particular job. His last job in the forces had been a thousand times harder.

No, this was *him*. Like it or not, he damned well was attracted to her and somehow he had to find a way to manage it without letting it affect their working relationship. It already was affecting it. Affecting him.

He expected his clients to obey him and his men without question. It was in the terms of any contract. Clients signed it knowing their lives were being placed in his hands. His clients, though, were, on the whole, heads of international organisations and other VIPs, the only common denominator between them being that they were travelling somewhere dangerous.

He had drilled it into his men that they were only employed for protection. They were not advisors or aides. Their client's business was not theirs.

The risks Francesca was taking by agreeing to

pay the bribe were none of his concern and she was correct that Pieta himself had paid them, although with far more discretion than she'd employed. Felipe had turned a blind eye to much worse before and had no doubt he would turn a blind eye to much worse in the future.

He couldn't fathom why it angered him so much to see her taking the kind of risks that had never concerned him from anyone else.

She'd turned up at his door while he'd been buck naked, her long hair damp, her beautiful face free from make-up, a long blue summer dress on with her pretty toes peeking out at the bottom and a hint of cleavage showing…

He'd become aroused just looking at her. He'd had to grip the door handle with one hand and press the wall tightly with the other to stop himself pulling her into his room and throwing her onto the bed.

This had only fired the anger already coursing through him.

After he'd closed the door he'd stood there for too long, not moving, just trying to quell his arousal, trying to ignore that her suite was adjacent to his.

A day off from her would be a blessing, especially as their time together had been extended to a whole week. He had to remember she was grieving and that grief made people act in wayward ways. She needed his help and support, not his condemnation and anger.

But God alone knew how he was going to cope with a week of her company without either throttling her or bedding her.

The early morning was so bright that one peek through the curtains lifted a little of the despondency in Francesca's heart. The hotel's ground staff were already up and about, weeding and watering the abundant blooming flowers, hosing the pathways, many yawning.

She yawned in sympathy but didn't consider going back to bed. More sleep was the last thing she wanted. Sleep brought dreams and the ones she'd had during the night were still horribly vivid. Pieta had been sitting at the small kitchen table in her apartment in Pisa. She'd made him a coffee and laughed as she'd told him she'd thought he'd died. He'd laughed too and said it had been a misunderstanding. And then he'd stopped laughing and said he knew the truth about how she'd reacted when told he'd died.

She'd awoken muttering into her sopping wet pillow that she was sorry, sorry, sorry, over and over.

For some reason Felipe had been in the background of those dreams too.

She wiped fresh tears away with the palm of her hand.

She needed to get a grip on herself and get her head back to where it had been before she'd fallen asleep with her face buried in the thick file Alberto had given her before she'd left Pisa. She'd sat on the huge bed to re-read it, determined that from now on all her actions would be above board. She would be prepared for any situation that came her way. She would not do anything else that could jeopardise her career or Pieta's foundation.

After dressing she made her way to the main hotel restaurant, where she was the first to be seated for breakfast. She didn't want to be on her own. She'd ordered room service the night before and stayed in her suite. Now she craved company.

There was no company to be found here, though. All the other guests were still sleeping. Even if they'd been up she would still have been alone. This wasn't a hotel for the solo traveller.

There was one other solo traveller staying here too, she reminded herself glumly, but he didn't want her company. He didn't even like her, that much was patently obvious.

And she didn't like him. The less she had to do with Felipe Lorenzi the happier she'd be and today she didn't have to deal with him at all.

She managed to avoid him until early afternoon.

She'd returned to her suite to start calling the names of the officials she'd need to meet for the hospital development. Half the numbers were either wrong or their phone lines had been disconnected by the hurricane. The others were, as Felipe had predicted, taking a day of rest and had no wish to speak to her, telling her to call back tomorrow. Only the Blue Train Aid Agency, the only aid agency to be up and running in Caballeros, had been available to talk. The worker she spoke to, Eva Bergen, had been full of enthusiasm for the project and readily agreed to meet her the next day. Eva's experience in the country would be tremendously useful and Francesca ended the call feeling much better about everything. So much better that she decided to buy a swimsuit from one of the hotel's exclusive boutiques and go for a swim.

There were four pools to choose from. Opting for the huge rectangular one, she swam a few laps then settled on a sun lounger with her book, shades on to keep the glare of the sun from her eyes.

But she couldn't settle. The words on the page blurred into a mass as she found her thoughts constantly drifting, not to the forthcoming week and everything it entailed but to her protector. In truth he'd been in her thoughts constantly.

She was glad of the book, though, when she spotted the tall figure in the tight black swim-shorts walk to the other side of the pool to where she lay, a towel slung over his shoulder.

If she wasn't already on hyper-alert to any sign of him she would still have noticed him. She doubted there was a woman poolside whose eye he didn't catch, young and old alike.

Quickly she raised her book so it covered her face, hoping it was enough to hide her.

Please don't let him see her.

The next time she faced him she wanted to be fully dressed and feeling confident in herself, not wearing a two-piece swimsuit that would put her at a further disadvantage.

Like it or not, she was stuck with him for the coming week and had no idea how she was going to get through it without slapping his arrogant, handsome face.

Pretending to be engrossed in her novel, she couldn't resist a surreptitious glance and found him at the edge of the pool, testing the temperature of the water with his toes.

Even with the distance between them his muscular beauty made her breath catch in her throat. All thoughts of hiding disappeared as she drank in the magnificence Felipe's clothing had only hinted at.

His darkly tanned skin gleamed under the bright afternoon sun, his chest broad and muscular, a light smattering of hair across the pecs thickening the lower they went over an abdomen she just *knew* would be hard to the touch.

With a grace that belied his size and muscularity, he dived in.

She heard the distinct sound of a woman sucking in a breath. It took a few beats to realise the sound had come from her.

His arms powered him to the far side then he rolled in the water and swam fluidly back.

Back and forth he went, streaking through the pool as if he'd been born to water, born to swim.

She couldn't tear her eyes from him. It was as if she'd been hypnotised.

She lost count of how many laps he swam before hauling himself out.

The ache that had steadily formed while she'd watched turned into a throb to see water drip from his body and she almost forgot she was trying to hide from him.

Shoving her book back over her face, she closed her eyes and took some long breaths in an attempt to get her heart rate back to one that didn't make her fear it would beat out of her chest.

Only when she opened her eyes again did she notice she was holding her book upside down. When she next peeked over it, Felipe had gone.

Fifty laps of the swimming pool and Felipe still felt wired.

Eight years in the forces had taught him to snatch sleep wherever he could. He'd slept without any problem leaning against jagged rocks, under prickly shrubs, in trenches of mud, with gun fire ringing in the distance, yet put him in a four-poster bed in a sweet-scented suite for a power nap and sleep remained stubborn. It had been stubborn all night.

It was that damned woman in the suite next door who was the cause of it.

He'd spent the morning working out tactics for the next few days, sending his plans over to James and Seb and his men situated on Caballeros.

He would feel better if he knew what those men who'd followed them had wanted but they'd proved harder to find than sleep.

Two more of his men were, at that moment, en route to Caballeros. When he returned there with Francesca in the morning there would be eyes and ears everywhere, keeping watch. Keeping her safe.

Felipe rubbed his eyes, sighed and swung his legs off the bed.

The guilt at his anger towards her had grown and his self-chastisement with it.

Control and discipline were the two most important elements needed for his job. He'd learned both in the forces and had carried it through to his business. He demanded the men he employed have the same qualities. When danger was rife, keeping a cool head was a necessity even when, as he'd learned to his bitter cost, it wasn't always enough.

He'd lost that cool head with Francesca.

He'd overstepped the mark. He would have to apologise. That had been his intention before he'd left his suite for a swim. He would do his fifty laps then seek her out and apologise.

She'd been at the poolside. He'd seen her the moment he'd stepped onto the tiles surrounding the pool, spotting her as she pulled a book over her face, pretending not to have seen him.

He'd swum his lengths with more vigour than usual, pounding the water as if the strokes could sweep away the image of Francesca on a recliner wearing nothing but a tiny pale yellow bikini.

Dios, she had curves that could make a man weep.

He'd sensed her watching his every stroke.

When he'd finished, he hadn't been able to resist another look while he'd dried himself. She'd been holding her book over her face again.

With the tell-tale tingles of arousal curling through his loins, he'd beaten a hasty retreat back to his suite and taken a cool shower.

Apologising could wait.

He couldn't entertain the thought of knocking on her suite door. That would be putting temptation in his path when he needed to divert around it.

It was standard practice to sleep in the adjacent room to the client. He'd arranged with the hotel manager to beef up the hotel's already tight security, the memory of the black Mondeo that had followed them hovering in the background of his mind a constant presence. Here, in this hotel, Francesca was safe. But not safe enough for him to contemplate changing suites to one on the other side of the complex, even though his every sinew strained to run.

Not wanting to be stuck with his own morose company and already bored with room service, he donned a pair of smart black chinos and a grey shirt, and decided to check out one of the hotel's many restaurants.

There were half a dozen eateries to choose from. The only one that appealed was the Mediterranean Restaurant and Bar, which seemed the most informal of them and promised live music.

If he could have chosen anywhere he would have found an American diner and eaten the largest burger on the menu but he didn't want to drive. He wanted to surround himself with people, eat and then sleep.

The restaurant was busy. A bar covered one wall while a small stage and dance area was set up on the wall opposite.

A waiter led him to an available table and as they went through the room Felipe spotted a lone figure sitting at a table tucked away in the corner, reading a menu.

His heart managed to sink and leap at the same moment, and in that same moment Francesca gazed absently around the room and found him. There was one quick blink before she put her head back down.

He rubbed the back of his neck. At the pool it had been easy for them both to pretend they hadn't see each other but now there was no avoiding her.

CHAPTER FIVE

'DO YOU WANT some company?' Felipe asked when he reached her. She wore a pretty floral dress with tiny straps. He caught a glimpse of thigh.

Francesca eyed him warily then gave a small nod.

He took the chair the waiter held out for him and sat down, noting the tall multi-coloured cocktail glass with an umbrella and straw in it. 'What are you drinking?'

'Tequila Sunrise. Do you want one?'

'I'll stick to beer. Have you ordered?'

'I'm still making my mind up.'

The waiter scuttled off to get Felipe's beer.

Opening his menu, he watched Francesca studiously read hers, her teeth gnawing at her bottom lip.

'Have you had a good day?' he asked conversationally.

She shrugged but didn't look at him, reaching

for her drink with a hand that shook. 'I've had worse.' She took a long drink through the straw.

'This isn't an easy time for you,' he observed, knowing it to be an understatement. She'd buried her brother only a few days before.

Her shoulders rose in another shrug and to his horror he watched her blink frantically in an attempt to hold back glistening tears.

She yanked her napkin and dabbed at her eyes, laughing morosely. 'Look, Felipe, you don't have to eat with me. I know you're just being polite. If you want to find another table, I won't care.'

'No.' Feeling like a complete ass, he ran his fingers through his hair and stared at her until she met his gaze. 'I'm sorry for the way I spoke to you.'

That surprised her. She took another drink of her cocktail, the light of the candle flickering off her eyes.

Eventually she said in a small voice, 'Have you spoken to Daniele about what happened yesterday with the Governor?'

'No.' He'd thought long and hard about it but had come to the conclusion that while she'd acted rashly, his condemnation had been too harsh. Francesca had been appalled when he'd pointed out the danger she'd put her career and the foundation in but it seemed she was far angrier with herself than he could be. She deserved the chance to see it through.

She closed her eyes. 'Thank you. I think I was overwrought yesterday. It's not an excuse but I've not been sleeping well since Pieta died and all that's been keeping me going is the thought of getting this hospital built. I promise I'll be considered in my approach from now on.'

'Why don't we draw a line through yesterday?' he suggested gently. 'Forget any cross words and start again?'

'I would like that,' she whispered. Reaching again for her napkin, she dabbed some more at her eyes then rolled her neck, took a deep breath, straightened and flashed him a smile that made his heart turn over. 'What are you going to eat? Seeing as Daniele's footing the bill, I'm going to select the most expensive items on the menu.'

Before he could correct her assumption, as he should have done the day before, she said, 'Have you met him?'

'Daniele?'

She nodded.

'I met him a few years ago in Paris with his girlfriend. Pieta introduced us.'

The bleak veil cloaking her since he'd joined her lifted in its entirety.

'Girlfriend? Daniele?' She leant forward, eyes alight. 'He's never had a girlfriend. Lots of scandalous flings, though.'

He shrugged. 'She was with him. I assumed she was his girlfriend. They acted like a couple.'

'Daniele with a girlfriend? That's amazing. Pieta knew they were together?'

'I assumed so.'

The waiter returned with Felipe's beer so they ordered their food and Francesca quickly finished her cocktail and ordered another.

'What were you all doing in Paris?' she asked when they were alone again.

'Attending a party at the US Embassy.'

'What did you think of Daniele?'

'Very different from Pieta.' He looked at her shrewdly. 'I would say you're more like him.'

'More like Daniele?'

'Pieta was intense and thoughtful.' At her darkening colour he added, 'You've an energy about you. You're impulsive and, I think, competitive. Daniele struck me as the same.'

She nodded slowly, her pupils moving fast as she thought. 'Yes. Daniele's highly competitive. He has to be first with everything and he *hates* losing.'

'And you? Am I right that you're also competitive?'

She grinned. 'I grew up wanting to be better than my brothers in everything.'

'Have you ever beaten them?'

'My aim throughout my education was to smash all their exam results.' She gave a mischievous smile. 'Which I achieved. It was very fulfilling. I even skipped a year. I like to tell people I'm the clever one of the family.'

Not so clever when it came to negotiating and agreeing bribes, he thought but didn't say. For the first time since they'd met they'd found relative harmony and he wasn't ready to break it.

'But when it comes to true competitiveness, Daniele's worse,' she continued. 'He's ferocious.'

'Has he always been like that?'

'As long as I've been alive. He grew up knowing the family wealth would pass on to Pieta—'

'*Only* to Pieta?'

'The oldest inherits the estate. It's always been

like that, for centuries. Pieta inherited when our father died.'

'What about your mother?'

'She has rights to the income during her lifetime but the physical assets transferred directly to Pieta.'

'Will it go to Daniele now?'

'Everything that's family wealth will so long as Natasha isn't pregnant.'

'Do you think she could be?'

'I don't know and none of us can bear to ask her. It would be cruel. We'll have to wait and see.'

'So if she is pregnant…?'

'Then we have the first in the next generation of Pellegrinis.' A sad smile played on her lips. 'If it's a boy he will inherit, if it's a girl then Daniele will inherit.'

'That doesn't sound fair.'

'Natasha will inherit Pieta's personal wealth whether she's pregnant or not. She will have enough to provide for a child and we will all love and cherish it whatever its gender.'

'And what do you get from your family estate?'

'Nothing.'

'That's not right either.'

'Right or not, that's how it is.'

'Doesn't it make you angry?' He didn't know why he was asking. Francesca's personal life was none of his concern.

Her second cocktail was brought to the table and she took it with a grateful smile and immediately sucked half of it up her straw. Done, she put the glass on the table. 'It's not just the wealth that's inherited, it's the responsibility. I was glad not to have it as it meant I could do whatever I wanted with my life without having to consider anyone else and, believe me, the life I've chosen is very different to the one expected for me.'

'In what way?'

She pulled a rueful face. 'I was expected to marry young and have babies, like all the women in my family have done for generations. It isn't supposed to matter that us weak females don't inherit anything because we're supposed to be provided for by our husbands.'

'You didn't want that?'

'I wanted to provide for myself and have a career, like my brothers.' The thought of being a kept woman filled Francesca with horror. Her mother had inherited money but had blithely given it to her husband to invest for her, believing herself too stupid to manage it herself.

She remembered being a small child and her mother casually asking her father for money to buy some new shoes. It had been a nothing incident, her father going straight into his wallet and handing the money over, but it had crystallised in Francesca's mind as the years passed. What if he'd said no? What would her mother have done then? Why should her mother not manage her own money? And why should she, Francesca, not be expected to go out and make a living of her own just because she was born a girl? Why could she not be like her brothers?

'I've no idea how Daniele will handle having the future of the Pellegrini family on his shoulders if it comes to it,' she carried on, shrugging off the old memories. 'He was so competitive with Pieta that he drove himself to make a fortune that was twice what Pieta would have inherited just to show that he could, but was able to live his life as he wanted without the responsibilities Pieta had. If he does inherit he'll have to marry so he'll say goodbye to his freedom too.'

Francesca's chest tightened, all this talk of her family reminding her of her mother stumbling at Pieta's funeral. She'd spoken to her briefly the night before, letting her know she'd arrived in the

Caribbean safely. Her mother had been too used to Francesca's stubbornness to try and talk her out of going but had made her swear she wouldn't put herself in any unnecessary danger.

'Forget your brothers, I'm curious about *you*. Do you even have a trust fund?'

'No, but all my education was paid for and I never wanted for anything when I was growing up. That's enough for me. I want to forge my own life.' One where she didn't have to ask for money to buy essentials.

'By following in Pieta's footsteps?' he said with obvious scepticism.

She paused, considering. 'There are—*were*—no better footsteps for me to follow in but don't think I wanted to make myself into his female clone. I saw the good Pieta was doing with his law degree and wanted to do it too.'

'Corporate law?'

She grimaced. 'No. I meant how he used it for the benefit of his philanthropy. Corporate law was a means to an end for him and that's what it is for me while I complete my traineeship.'

'What will you do when you're fully qualified?'

'I'm going to specialise in human rights.' She looked back up at him, straining to stifle the lump pressing in her chest. 'Can we stop talking about me and my family now? Just talk about nonsense? Otherwise I'm going to embarrass both of us by crying.'

A couple of hours later, Francesca's belly was full and her melancholy gone. The quick meal she'd intended to have before retiring to the unwelcome solitude of her suite had extended over three courses.

As time had passed, her animosity towards Felipe had melted, which she thought the handful of cocktails she'd consumed *might* have helped with.

A jazz band was playing on the stage, thankfully uplifting tunes, and there was a buzzing atmosphere she'd enthusiastically embraced. After the trauma of the past week it felt good to be letting her hair down. The gorgeous company helped.

Felipe was proving to be not quite the dictator she'd painted in her mind. But still arrogant, although not in the entitled way most men she'd come across in her life were. Felipe's arrogance came with an authority earned and built over an adulthood of having orders obeyed without question.

His apology had shocked her. She'd never known a man to apologise before, was quite sure the word 'sorry' didn't exist in any of the male Pellegrinis' vocabulary. Or her own, she had to admit.

She thought the more of him for it. A man who could hold his hands up when he was in the wrong without emasculating himself only soared in her estimation.

Francesca knew she could be pig-headed. It wasn't a part of her character she liked and, while in her head she would want to be saying sorry for whatever mishap or argument she'd caused or contributed to, her tongue would stubbornly resist.

Idly she wondered if Felipe's authority extended to the bedroom. What sort of lover would he be? She'd seen hints of fire beneath the calm, authoritative exterior—that fire had been aimed firmly at herself—and imagining those strong hands touching her made her skin tingle. What would it be like to have those intense dark eyes staring into hers in the height of passion…? Her lower belly clenched just to imagine it, the intensity of it shocking her.

She'd never had thoughts like these before.

Once their desserts were cleared away she ordered them Irish coffees.

She laughed at his arched eyebrow. 'It's not that late,' she defended.

'I'm more concerned about your head in the morning.'

She waved a hand airily. 'My head will be fine. I've not drunk that much.'

He fixed her with a stare that made her laugh when it should have quelled her.

'I might have drunk a little more than is good for me but I'm not drunk. And you've had as many as me.'

'I'm twice your size and have a much greater tolerance.'

'You are *huge*,' she agreed, leaning over to put a hand on his bare forearm. 'I bet you work out a lot.'

'Whenever I can.'

The dark hairs resting under her fingers were much finer than she'd expected, his skin smooth and warm.

'Are you married?' she asked impulsively.

'No.' Felipe moved his arm away from her touch and drained the last of his beer.

Her touch had felt too good for comfort.

'Have you ever been married?'

'No.'

'Ever come close to getting married?'

'No.'

'Do you have a girlfriend?'

He sighed. His love life was not a discussion he wanted with Francesca.

He should have gone to bed a long time ago.

'No. There's no room in my life for a relationship.'

'No room in your life? What a strange thing to say.'

Their Irish coffees were laid before them. Francesca popped two sugar cubes into hers and gave it a vigorous stir.

'That spoils it,' he reproached. 'See? You've mixed the cream into it.'

'I need the sweetness.'

She would taste sweet. His weak-willed imagination that couldn't stop picturing her in that damned bikini was certain of it.

'Why is there no room for you to have a relationship? Do you need a bigger house?'

He almost laughed at the wink she finished her question with. As the evening had progressed she'd relaxed, her antagonism towards him now but a memory. Francesca had proven to be fun company, far removed from the spoilt brat he'd assumed her to be.

He had to keep reminding himself that she was his client—a grieving, vulnerable client—and that he needed to keep his guard up. This wasn't a date. It wouldn't end with a nightcap in one of their suites followed by…

He refused to allow his mind to wander any further.

'It's my life as a whole. When my job with you is over I'm going back to the Middle East and then on to Russia. I run a business with three hundred employees. It takes a lot of management.'

'Why does that stop you having a relationship?'

'I doubt there's a woman out there who would be happy with a man she went months at a time without seeing and weeks without any communication at all.'

'Natasha and Pieta often went months without seeing each other,' she pointed out. 'It didn't do them any harm and they were together for years.'

That's what she thought.

But Felipe wouldn't say anything negative about her brother when his coffin had only just been lowered into the ground. One day the truth he suspected—and he had no proof, only a gut instinct—about her brother would come out as the truth always did. He just hoped she was in the right mental space to cope with it when it did.

'Pieta was a very different man to me and when I disappear it's usually into danger. My business comes first. It has to. My men are deployed to the world's most dangerous hotspots where situations are fluid. Every eventuality has to be catered for. A call can come in at any time for an evacuation.'

'What if something were to go wrong with one of the jobs while you're here dining with me?' she asked reasonably.

He held his phone up. 'This is a satellite phone. It's standard military issue. All my men have one. They allow us to communicate with each other wherever we are in the world and the encryption means no one can hack them.'

'So if one of your clients or men were to get into trouble right now, you'd sort it all out sitting here with me?'

'My headquarters are manned twenty-four seven. There are protocols in place for every eventuality. But if anything untoward *were* to happen I'd be kept informed throughout.' Situations happened all the time. It was the nature of the job. People needed his protection for very good reasons and they hired his firm because they were guaranteed the best. In the ten years since he'd formed the firm, no client had ever come to harm.

'But if anything were to happen right now, you wouldn't personally be involved with solving it,' she persisted. 'So if you have the staff in place to keep everything running during your absences, there's nothing to stop you having a relationship.'

'I'm only ever absent from headquarters when I'm on a job. Being the boss means having all the responsibility if anything goes wrong.' He would not allow anything to go wrong.

Her eyes narrowed then began to dance. 'You sound like a man making excuses. Has a woman broken your heart?'

'No woman has ever got close.' And no woman ever would. During his army career he'd been happy to play the field—many women loved a man in uniform. He'd watched friends and colleagues settle down and seen the pressure starting families had had on them, how it could affect their focus and priorities, and had decided to wait until he left the forces before finding someone to settle down with. Then his unit had been flown in to handle a hostage situation, his life had gone to hell and thoughts of a family destroyed with it. He was better off on his own. Solitude was what he'd grown up with, what he was used to. Safer.

He thought of Sergio. He thought of Sergio's wife and unborn child. He thought about the hostages they'd been trying to save, half of whom hadn't made it out alive. Sergio hadn't made it out alive either, a memory that still had the power to sear him. His child was now a healthy nine-year-old growing up with a father he would only see in photographs.

Francesca didn't say anything, just stared at him with those beguiling light brown eyes that seemed to drink him in…

Without warning, she got to her feet, her face breaking into a beaming smile. 'I love this song! Let's dance.'

The jazz band had finished their set and now a DJ was playing to the full crowd.

'I don't dance.'

'Then I shall dance on my own.' And with that she finished her coffee and glided to the dance floor, her shoulders and hips swaying to the music he vaguely recognised, her long ebony hair shimmering in the lights.

Without an ounce of self-consciousness, Francesca threw her arms in the air and began to dance. The joy on her face must have been infectious because a couple of women hurried onto the floor to join her, the three of them immediately dancing and singing together as if they'd known each other for years.

He should leave her on the dance floor and go to bed. He wasn't her babysitter. His protection of her did not involve making sure she was safely tucked up at night. Judging by the animation on her face and in her body she'd found her second wind and wouldn't be going to bed any time soon.

Felipe sighed and signalled to a passing waiter for another beer.

He couldn't leave her.

And neither could he take his eyes from her.

He accepted his beer with a nod of thanks.

He sipped it slowly, watching her dance.

How could someone be so uninhibited? Did it come naturally to her or was it something she'd forced herself to be? He suspected it was the former, that this woman on the dance floor was the closest to the real Francesca he'd seen in their short time together.

It felt as if he'd been in her company for weeks.

She kept glancing at him, sometimes overtly, beckoning him with a finger to join her, to which he always shook his head.

Hell would freeze over before he'd dance with anyone, let alone Francesca Pellegrini. Watching her move and imagining her body flush against his own was enough torture to inflict on himself.

And sometimes her glances were fleeting, as if she couldn't help but look. Just as he couldn't help but look at her.

He shifted in his seat then smiled sardonically when a waiter brought the three dancing ladies a cocktail each. So much for his keen attention to detail—he'd no idea how or when she'd ordered them but seeing as they were Tequila Sunrises, he knew damn well they'd come from Francesca.

She met his eye again and winked, then drank her cocktail and returned to dancing with gusto.

The bubble of laughter swelling inside him died on his lips when one of her straps fell down her slender arm. She giggled and pulled it up, only for it to fall straight back down again.

The attraction Felipe had been trying to contain all night seemed to burst through him, the pulsing music dimming to a background noise as blood roared through his ears.

Shoving his chair back, he got to his feet.

It was time to call it a night before he did something he regretted, like joining Francesca on the dance floor and holding her so close she'd be able to feel his desire for herself.

CHAPTER SIX

FELIPE MADE IT out of the restaurant and was halfway across the atrium when he heard light footsteps behind him.

'You left without me!' she accused.

He closed his eyes tightly and prayed for strength.

When he opened them he found Francesca's beautiful face gazing up at him, her skin glowing from her exertion on the dance floor. She didn't look upset at him leaving. If anything, she looked far too knowing.

'We weren't on a date and it's late,' he felt compelled to remind her. And remind himself. When she looked at him like that…

'Have I annoyed you again?'

He could laugh at her lack of guile. How many times had he heard his colleagues complain that women never made it easy for them, always expecting them to read their minds and know when something was wrong rather than just coming out and saying it? There was none of that with Francesca. Her emotions were always on the surface.

'No, you haven't annoyed me.'

'Good.' She tucked her arm through his. 'Then you can walk me back to my room.'

If she didn't look so unsteady on her feet he would shake her off.

He was annoyed enough with himself for allowing their meal drag on so long and for hanging around to watch her dance when he should have taken the earliest opportunity to escape.

His heart sinking in rhythm with his warming skin, Felipe took a deep breath and led the way.

'I've had a wonderful evening,' she said. 'Thank you for keeping me company.'

'No problem.'

'And you?' When he didn't answer, she prompted, 'Have you had a nice evening?'

That was a question he was not prepared to answer with anything more than a noncommittal grunt.

Thankfully they'd reached her door, allowing him to remove his arm from her hold and step back.

She rummaged in her bag and found her key card and immediately dropped it.

'Oops.'

'I'll get it,' he muttered.

He scooped it up and swiped the lock for her, then opened the door.

'Do you want to come in?'

He shook his head.

'The bar's got beer in it,' she said temptingly.

'I've had enough to drink.' He'd drunk only half of what she had but, as he'd reminded himself a dozen times throughout their meal, he was working. All that dancing had probably worked a lot of the alcohol out of her system but she was by no means sober. And she'd had the extra cocktail on the dance floor…

Yes, there was no way she was sober. Felipe was used to drinking with hardened men, not slender—but curvy, *Dios*, he could not get those curves out of his mind—women.

She bit her lip then tilted her head. 'Don't you find me attractive?'

God give him strength.

'I need to get some sleep.'

'You haven't answered my question. You didn't answer my last question either.'

The strap of her dress fell down again. He

spoke through gritted teeth. 'I'm not going to answer it.'

Heavy footsteps trod towards them. He turned to see a man around his own age heading their way.

'Get into your room.' Felipe took hold of her wrist and walked her in. He didn't want to advertise the fact she would be alone in her suite.

The door closed quietly behind them.

Resolutely, he kept his back pressed against it. He would count to ten and then leave.

One. Two. Three.

'You *do* find me attractive,' she whispered, eyes shining as she stood before him.

Four. Five. Six.

She raised herself onto her toes and palmed his cheeks with hands as soft as anything he'd ever felt. 'I find you attractive too,' she breathed.

Seven. Eight…

He lost the count when her breath danced over his lips and her mouth found his.

Holding his breath, he clenched his hands into fists and willed himself not to respond.

He couldn't. He mustn't.

Francesca's lips didn't move. Not for a long time. He felt her breathe him in and fought not to inhale. Then she did move. Just a little. A turn of her head to cover his mouth better, a gentle, tentative exploration of his lips while her fingers made a gentle, tentative exploration of his cheeks and jaw, rubbing against his beard and up to trace the contours of his ears.

He fought to hold on, fought to deny the sensation burning through him.

He might have won had he not opened his mouth to let in air and her tongue darted through his parted lips. In an instant he was filled with the sweet heat of her kiss and the fingers he'd raised to yank her hands away from him were cradling her skull as he kissed her back as deeply as a parched man drinking from a cup.

She tasted sweeter than he could have dreamed.

Her arms wrapped around his neck while his arm hooked around her waist to crush her to him. She melted into him with a breathy sigh, charging his desire like a rocket.

He roamed her curves, finding her waist, her hips, her bottom, which was round and pert and felt delectable beneath his fingers. *She* was delectable. Soft and womanly beyond imagination.

Rising onto her toes had the effect of lifting her dress. When he skimmed down her thigh he came to bare skin that had him sucking in a breath at its satin sheen and holding her tightly so he could devour her mouth again.

It was her response that so blew his mind. Her hunger was as acute as his own and it fed his.

He could take her now if he wanted and she would welcome him with the breathy sighs that were growing in intensity. God knew, he wanted to take her, this craving like nothing he had ever known.

His exploring hands ran up her bare thighs to find her panties and he slipped a finger under the skimpy material and almost groaned aloud to feel the hot dampness there.

She squirmed against him, one foot running up and down the length of his leg, kissing him, licking him, her teeth grazing his neck then kissing up to brush her cheeks against his beard like a purring cat. He could taste her desire in her kisses, smell it in the heat radiating off her.

Tugging the panties down her hips, he pressed the palm of his hand over the soft, downy hair and felt the gasp that flew from her throat. She pressed her pubis into him but before he could explore any further, her nails suddenly dug through his shirt and into his flesh and she collapsed into him, crying out and shuddering.

And then she stilled.

For a long, drawn out moment Felipe couldn't find his breath. Francesca didn't seem to be breathing either.

The only sound he heard with any clarity was the roar of blood in his ears.

It was like the room was clearing of fog. Slowly they released their hold on each other and took wary steps back.

What the hell did he think he was playing at? Had he lost his mind?

Francesca put trembling hands to her mouth, covering it as if in prayer, her eyes wide and dazed.

He felt pretty dazed himself.

He breathed out deeply.

He'd been minutes away from making love to her. There were no excuses he could make.

For the first time in his life he'd let his desire guide him and his loathing for himself tasted like salt on his tongue.

He was a thirty-six-year-old man. He knew better than this. He *demanded* better than to behave like this.

He should never have followed her into the suite, not when his awareness of her and the desire in his loins had been simmering since the first moment he'd set eyes on her.

'I need to go.'

She jerked her head and took another step back. He took it as agreement.

His heart hammering, he backed away to the door and left.

Francesca put the pillow over her head to drown out the sound of the knocking on the door. She knew who it was and she did not want to see him. She didn't want to see him ever again. She couldn't. It was just too mortifying.

She'd rather dance naked through the streets of Caballeros with the lecherous Governor ogling her than see Felipe again.

Her cheeks scalded to remember how she'd come undone with one touch.

One touch.

Why didn't she know that could happen? How *could* she have known when she hadn't even kissed a man before?

His *face*. He'd been horrified.

No wonder he'd run from her suite.

And to think she'd gone into the restaurant hating him.

She'd just wanted to kiss him.

It was his smile that had done it, one unguarded curve of those gorgeous lips that had made her own lips tingle and her pulses quicken.

She'd spent almost their entire meal fantasising about the feel of his lips on hers.

Curiosity had certainly killed the cat.

She couldn't even blame it on the alcohol, although she wished she could. It had loosened her inhibitions considerably but she'd been the one to drive the kiss, not the Tequila Sunrises.

She'd played with fire and been burnt for her trouble. She certainly wouldn't open the door to the man who'd lit it.

The phone beside her bed rang.

She wanted to scream. *Just leave me alone!*

She snatched the receiver up. 'What?'

'You have one minute to open your door or I break it down.'

The dial tone played out before she could summon the words to answer back.

Throwing on her robe, she hurried to open the door a crack before Felipe could follow up on his threat.

He was already there.

He didn't wait for an invite, simply pushed the door open and strode in, glass of fizzing water in hand.

'Drink that,' he said, handing it to her. 'It'll help your hangover.'

'I don't have a hangover.' She was quite sure the sickness in her belly was nothing to do with alcohol. Her banging head might be, though.

'Just drink it.'

How could he look so fresh? He'd showered, his charcoal suit crisply pressed, his hair still damp.

Sulkily, she did as she was told and gulped the liquid down. It tasted much less disgusting than she expected.

He took a deep breath. 'May I sit down?'

No. Go away and let me sleep away my mortification. 'If you want.'

He sat on the armchair in the corner and indicated for her to sit on the sofa.

Perching herself gingerly, aware of the humiliation ravaging her, she tried to put on a brave face. Tried to show she didn't care what he thought of her.

But she did care. She really did.

'I must apologise for my behaviour last night,'

he said heavily. 'I should never have taken advantage of you as I did.'

The last thing she'd expected was an apology.

His choice of words made her study him properly.

Her heart loosened to see he wasn't angry with her. Felipe's anger was directed at himself.

His self-recrimination also loosened her tongue. 'You didn't take advantage of me. If anything I took advantage of you. I started it.'

'You were drunk,' he refuted flatly.

'Not drunk enough that I didn't know what I was doing.'

Heat pulsed between her thighs as she remembered how wonderful it had been in that moment and how she'd ached to do so much more. She'd had no idea such feelings existed in her. Desire and curiosity had erupted into something she'd had no control over.

And he'd been a full participant. She'd been so busy castigating herself and so busy focussing on his abrupt departure from her suite that she'd pushed aside *his* response. She might not have had any prior experience but she'd felt his arousal pressed hard against her belly and known what it meant. He'd wanted her as much as she'd wanted him.

He dug his fingers into the back of his skull, a set look in his jaw. 'I run my company with strict rules. No relations with the client.'

'Is that what you call it? *Relations*?'

'We both know what it means.' Now he pressed his hand to his forehead. 'It's not just the rules I abide by. It's you. You're too young to be messing around with men old enough to be your…'

'Big brother?' she supplied.

His jaw clenched. 'Francesca, you are in my care for a very good reason. You're too young and too vulnerable to be party to a tawdry affair.'

'My mother got married at nineteen. She was pregnant with Pieta when she was my age. If my family had had their way, I would be married with kids by now. If I want to be party to a tawdry affair, then I'm more than old enough to make that choice.'

'But you *are* vulnerable and grieving. You can't argue with that.' He got to his feet. 'You're my client. There can be nothing between us. Do you understand that?'

She stared at him for a long time, taking in the

tension radiating from him. He hadn't looked her in the eye since entering her suite.

'Answer me one thing,' she said. 'One of the questions I asked last night, and this time I want an answer. Are you attracted to me?'

'Whatever attraction I feel is irrelevant,' he answered roughly.

'It wasn't irrelevant last night.'

'Last night was a mistake that will not be repeated.'

'Says you?'

Jaw clenched, he strode to the door. 'This conversation is over. If you still want to visit the hospital site and meet up with the charity, then I suggest you get dressed. We leave in thirty minutes.'

He left her suite without further comment.

Alone, Francesca drew her knees to her chin and hugged her legs. She felt she could start dancing again.

For all her fears that she'd made another monumental mistake, Felipe *did* desire her and that knowledge took away the sting of his rejection. If he'd flat-out denied it she thought it possible she might be tempted to curl into hedgehog-like ball and hibernate until she could be sure of looking at him without toe-curling shame and embarrassment. That the attraction was mutual made it a whole lot easier to bear even if he was adamant that last night was a one off.

Eventually she straightened and took some long breaths, forcing herself to concentrate on what was important. She was in the Caribbean for a reason and that reason wasn't for a holiday or for a man.

The woman she was meeting from the Blue Train Agency had promised to discuss the hospital, the needs of the people and how Francesca should navigate her way around the additional bureaucracy she would find.

She needed to be alert and have her professional head on, not be fantasising about what it would take to wear down Felipe's defences.

The day passed quickly and much more productively than Francesca could have hoped. Eva Bergen from the Blue Train Agency had been there to meet her at Caballeros' airport, as she'd promised, escorted by a couple of Felipe's men, and they'd spent the day visiting the site where they hoped to build the hospital and met some of the officials she'd have to deal with when the site was signed over to Pieta's foundation on Saturday. After arranging meetings with the other officials for the next day, they headed back to Aguadilla.

When they dropped Seb and James off at their lodging, she stayed in the back of the car to make more calls without the distraction of Felipe's strong thighs in her eyeline.

Her first call was to Alberto. It went to voicemail.

'Problem?' Felipe asked from the driver's seat when she cursed under her breath, adopting the same grim tone he'd used since he'd left her suite that morning.

Clearly his regret of their *relations* meant he was now determined to keep his distance as much as the situation allowed. Today he'd left it to Seb to stand at her side as principal protection but had still been close enough to listen in on every conversation, close enough to ward off any perceived threat that might come her way.

Not once had he met her eye.

In a way she was grateful for his distance as it had allowed her to concentrate on what needed doing.

'I've been trying to get hold of Alberto to arrange for the cash to be sent over in time for the

Governor's party,' she explained. 'He'll know what to do about the bribe too without getting the foundation into trouble but he's not answering his phone.'

Until everything was sorted out with Pieta's estate and businesses, Alberto controlled the finances for the foundation. When she'd spoken to him at Pieta's funeral he'd assured her he would sign off the funds when a deal was brokered.

'It's already in hand,' Felipe informed her. 'My men will transport it. The money arrives in Aguadilla on Saturday.'

'How do you know that?'

'I made the arrangements.'

'What? *When*?'

'Yesterday.'

'But… How…? Why?' She couldn't get a coherent question to form.

'I decided the best way to get you out of the mess you'd got yourself into was to sort it out myself before you dragged yourself in deeper.'

It took a long time for Francesca to find her voice. 'This has nothing to do with you. You're here as my protection…'

'Exactly. A young woman with a suitcase of cash? Four hundred thousand dollars is a fortune to the people of Caballeros. You'll be a magnet for every thief out there and you're already a target.'

'How's anyone going to know about the money?' she protested. 'It's a private transaction between myself and the Governor.'

'A private transaction—or bribe—agreed in a residence I warned you was filled with cameras recording every word you said. This is damage limitation. The cash for the site will be paid in full from the foundation but the bribe money will come from a different source. There will be no trail leading it to you or your brother's foundation.'

'You've done all this? The damage limitation?'

'Yes. Don't ask me how. I have no wish to lie to you.'

Francesca clenched her hands into fists and forced herself to breathe. She knew she should be grateful to him for saving her from herself, not wanting to bash him over the head with her handbag.

'I thank you for thinking of my career.' She spoke carefully, struggling for breath. 'But don't ever go over my head like that again. If anything else occurs, speak to me before acting.'

'If you'd been thinking clearly in the first place I wouldn't have had to go over your head.'

'That was then,' she contested tightly. 'What happened to drawing a line under it all? I made one mistake...'

'My actions prevented you making another.'

'I made one mistake that I'm doing my best not to repeat and it's not fair to keep throwing it in my face. Have *you* never made a mistake? Or were you born perfect?'

He didn't answer.

They drove the rest of the route back to the hotel in silence and went to their respective suites without a further word.

CHAPTER SEVEN

FRANCESCA CLOSED THE folder sprawled on her lap with a sigh and rubbed her eyes. It was gone midnight. She'd been in her suite since their return to the hotel, having another re-read of the foundation's files. She wished she'd brought some of the case files she was supposed to be studying for her traineeship with her, could kick herself for not even thinking about it. When she returned home to Pisa she would get her head down and get stuck back into her studies.

In the hours spent reading, she'd ordered room service and drunk nothing stronger than black coffee but even all the caffeine couldn't stop the heaviness of her eyes. All those Tequila Sunrises from the night before had finally caught up with her. She was exhausted.

She really needed to get some sleep but was terrified of closing her eyes, wondered if there was some magic pill out there that guaranteed a dreamless sleep.

Her thoughts, as always, drifted back to Felipe. As the night had gone on her fury at his high-handed behaviour had slowly evaporated.

She wondered where he was. Had he left his suite that evening or stayed in as she had done? The hotel's walls were so solid that no sound penetrated.

On impulse she leaned over, picked up the telephone receiver from the bedside table and dialled his room number.

He answered on the second ring. 'Yes?'

'It's me. Francesca Pellegrini.'

She pulled a disgusted face at herself. Why did she give him her *surname*?

There was a small pause before he said, a slight tinge of amusement in his voice, 'What can I do for you, Francesca Pellegrini?'

His words sounded like a caress. He really had the dreamiest of voices.

'I wanted to say thank you…for digging me out of the hole I'd put myself and the foundation in… and…and…' She forced the word out. 'Sorry… for being so ungrateful about it.'

'Apology accepted.'

'Just like that?'

'Just like that.'

'You don't want me to crawl over broken glass to show my penitence?'

A low rumble of laughter blew into her ear and curled its way down her spine. 'An apology is enough. I'm not without blame. You weren't being ungrateful. You were right to be angry with me. I should have consulted with you before I went ahead with my plans.'

'Why didn't you?'

'I was angry with you and the whole situation. I thought you'd behaved insanely.'

'I *did* behave insanely,' she conceded. 'Do you normally try and fix the holes your clients dig for themselves?'

A small pause. 'No.'

'Do you often get angry with your clients?'

Another small pause. 'No. It's not my place to get angry with them or fix their problems. I'm paid to protect them, not have an opinion.'

His confession made the most wonderful warmth spread through her. She pulled her knees up and curled against the headboard and murmured, 'I must be special then.'

Another rumble of laughter. 'That is one way to describe you.'

'Am I the most annoying client you've ever had?'

'You're the most challenging,' he answered drily.

'I've always been challenging.'

'I'll bet.'

A silence formed.

'It's late. I should let you go,' she said, breaking it. But she didn't want to let him go. She wanted to have that glorious voice speak into her ear all night. A thought occurred to her. 'Did I wake you?'

'I'm watching a film in bed.'

'Is it any good?'

'It's bad enough to remind me why I hate television.'

'You can't hate television,' she said, feigning outrage.

He groaned. 'Don't tell me you're one of those television addicts?'

'I *love* television,' she informed him gleefully. 'If I was put on a desert island and only allowed to take one thing that would be it.'

'You're a heathen.'

'A heathen with a large collection of box sets.'

His laughter rumbled down the line again,

warming her from her lobes all the way down to her toes.

To think Felipe was lying in his bed too…

'Did you go anywhere for dinner?' she asked.

'I had room service in my suite.'

'So did I.'

'What did you have?'

'Jambalaya. You?'

'The same.'

There was no reasonable answer as to why Felipe independently eating the same meal as her should make her glow.

Another silence formed, this time broken by Felipe. 'We should get some sleep.'

'I'm not tired.' A lie. She was exhausted. But speaking to Felipe had recharged her. She wanted more than a conversation down the phone. The easiness of their talk, the subtle undertones racing beneath it propelled her to say, 'Do you want to come to my suite for a nightcap?'

There was another prolonged pause with time enough to make her heart expand with anticipation.

'Goodnight, Francesca,' he eventually said in such a gentle tone her heart flipped over on itself and her unanswered offer didn't sting as much as it should.

She hugged the receiver to her chest for a long time after he'd hung up.

When Felipe strode into the hotel lobby the next morning, the first person he saw was Francesca, sitting on a sofa with her legs elegantly crossed, reading a newspaper.

As if she had a sixth sense to his presence, she tilted her head and immediately fixed her gaze on him. Her lips curved into a smile that made his chest compress.

He nodded a greeting in return.

He'd given himself a sharp talking to that morning, reminding himself of all the reasons he needed to keep his distance from this mesmeric woman. He'd put the phone down after their late-night conversation with an ache in his groin that had still been there when he'd woken.

Her call had caught him off guard. Her husky voice had played down the line, into his ear and into his veins before he could put the mental blocks in place to deflect it.

Her apology had taken him off guard too. Francesca was not a woman who found apologies easy.

That he knew such a thing about her disturbed him on many different levels but nowhere near as disturbing as the strength it had taken to refuse her suggestive offer of a nightcap. He hadn't been able to refuse in words, not when his tongue had been clamouring with the rest of his body to say yes.

He should have ended the call after she'd made her apology, not allowed that husky voice draw him into further, more intimate conversation.

They had five more days left together and in one respect he was glad they would now be able to get through it without a wishing well full of antagonism between them.

He could laugh at his optimism. He'd only known her a short time but knew perfectly well Francesca was not a woman one could expect to have an easy life with, not even for five short days. Everything she did, she did with passion. Everything she felt was with passion.

He'd felt that passion for himself and, *Dios*, he craved to feel it again.

He'd never met anyone like her. He'd never desired anyone as he did her. He'd never become aroused at a voice before.

He'd had to force himself to say goodnight.

'Ready to go?' he said briskly. He would not allow the spell they'd fallen into during their late-night call seep into the job in hand.

It had been one phone call, he told himself irritably. They'd hardly shared a naked sauna together.

But, naturally, his thoughts immediately turned to the image permanently lodged in his retinas of her sunbathing in that tiny yellow bikini.

Thankfully, today she was fully covered in a simple blue knee-length dress, black fitted jacket and black heels, her dark hair plaited and coiled. She looked ready to step into a courtroom. She also looked as sexy as a siren.

Her light brown eyes widened a little at his tone but her poise remained. 'I'm ready when you are.'

They collected Seb and James at their lodgings and then drove onto the airport, keeping conversation light and professional. If not for the gleam in her eyes every time she looked at him he could believe he'd mistaken the sensual undertone in her nightcap offer. But the gleam shone brightly.

She shone brightly even though she was more together and composed than he had ever seen her.

When she met with the official in charge of the island's medical service, who in turn expected his own bribe, he was impressed with the way she used a combination of facts, charm and intelligence to deflect him and get him to agree to naming a wing of the hospital after him in lieu of a backhander.

'Weren't you tempted to use that technique when dealing with the Governor?' he asked on the drive back to the airport.

She shook her head and pulled her lips together ruefully. 'I wish that meeting could be scrubbed away so I could pretend it never happened. I was so excited to get his agreement that, frankly, if he'd asked me to serve him the moon on a dish I would have accepted. I didn't think the ramifications through clearly. I should have been a lot more prepared.'

He admired her ability not to pull punches at her own faults. The more he observed her, the more he found to admire, from her professionalism to that inherent zest for life she carried with her. 'You didn't make the same mistake this time.'

She met his eye and her lips curved. 'I make it a point to learn from my mistakes, not repeat them.'

That was so close to his own personal beliefs that for a moment he was tempted to pull her to him…

Ever since those crazy, heady few minutes in her suite he'd done his damnedest not to think of it, not to remember the sweet heat of her passionate kisses or the softness of her lips and silkiness of her skin. It was the cry of surprise she'd made when she'd come with virtually one touch that he couldn't eradicate. Remembering that sound made his every sinew tighten.

He knew he could never make the mistake of being alone in a room with her again.

'Boss?'

James's voice broke into his thoughts. They'd pulled into Caballeros airport where the pilot was waiting for them. 'Yes?'

'See that black Mondeo?'

Felipe followed his gaze. Roughly ten metres away from their Cessna sat the car that had followed them from the Governor's house three days ago.

He thought quickly as he scanned their surroundings.

'Stay here,' he told Francesca before getting out of the car. Seb and James, who'd already recognised the danger and armed themselves, didn't need to be told to stay with her or to keep the engine running.

Gun in hand, keeping the black car in his eyeline, he strolled with deceptive casualness to the Cessna. If this was an ambush he wouldn't have Francesca caught in any crossfire.

'How long has that Mondeo been there?' he asked his man who he'd left with the pilot.

'Three hours. Three men.'

'Any activity?'

'None. I've run a trace on the licence plate but you know what this island's like—even before the hurricane I doubt I'd have got any information from it. We're working on facial recognition as we speak.'

Felipe nodded grimly and said to the pilot, 'Get ready to leave.'

The small plane's engine was switched on before his feet hit the tarmac and he was heading back to Francesca.

'What's going on?' she asked when he opened

the car door. 'Is it the men who were following us before?'

'It appears so.' He held out his hand, preparing to throw her over his shoulder if she gave any resistance. 'Time to move.'

He gave her credit. She didn't hesitate or demand more answers. Her eyes held his—he could almost read her thoughts, Francesca saying 'Okay, I'm trusting you here,'—and she took his hand and held it tightly on the quick march back to the plane, James flanking her other side, Seb bringing up the rear.

Only when they were seated, their belts hardly buckled before the pilot had them airborne, did she quietly say, 'I assume those men mean trouble.'

'I have to assume that too.'

She nodded slowly. 'Them being at the airport can't be a coincidence. What do you think they want?'

'That's the million dollar question.' A question he'd give one of his kidneys to answer.

She didn't speak for the longest time. 'Do you think they know about the money?'

'I would put my savings on it.' He wiped perspiration from his brow. He already knew what he would have to do.

Unbuckling himself, he moved to the front of the plane to share his thoughts with his men.

He waited until they arrived at James and Seb's lodgings and the two men had got out of the car before sharing it with Francesca. She'd proved remarkably stoical about the situation. He must have made a dozen phone calls and she'd sat quietly beside him, not interrupting, not talking, letting him get on with what he needed to do.

'James and Seb are getting their gear together. They're coming with us.'

'To our hotel?'

'I've also arranged for three of my men staying in Caballeros to fly here. Between them they'll cover all entry points to the hotel and keep watch.' Now that the threat against Francesca was unequivocal he would not trust her safety in the hotel to the security guards. Guards could be bribed. His men could not. His men wouldn't miss anything.

The face she pulled was sceptical. 'You think those men at the airport are going to come here?'

'I don't know what those men are going to do so I'm preparing for any eventuality.'

'Aguadilla has really tight security. Our hotel has really tight security. They haven't got a hope of getting to us.'

'You may be right but I'm not taking any risks.' He wasn't prepared to leave anything to chance. Security at Aguadilla airport was as tight as any in the US or Europe, its waters heavily patrolled. In theory Francesca should be safe for as long as she remained in Aguadilla. In theory.

Felipe had learned a long time ago that 'in theory' didn't mean a damn thing. People were unpredictable, especially those under pressure.

His gut told him it was the money the men were after and not Francesca personally. They'd initially followed them from the Governor's residence. That had to mean they'd been tipped off about the money from a member of the Governor's personal staff.

But what if he was wrong? What if they wanted both, the cash *and* a hostage for ransom?

What if they weren't merely staking them out, waiting for signs of the cash, and were instead only waiting for an opportunity to snatch her? He'd been at the forefront of a hostage situation that had gone wrong. The thought of Francesca being held…

His stomach roiled violently.

He'd watched the light die in Sergio's eyes and the eyes of his other fallen comrades. He could not allow himself to imagine it draining from Francesca's eyes too. To protect her and keep her safe he had to keep his focus.

There were too many what-ifs. Far too many.

Francesca was quite sure she should be biting her nails in terror. That would be a normal reaction to being followed by unknown persons on one of the most dangerous islands in the world.

But she was safe in Aguadilla with Felipe and his army of warriors protecting her. Unlike Caballeros, Aguadilla was a true paradise.

She'd definitely experienced fear when she'd realised the men who'd followed them after her meeting with the Governor had been staking out their Cessna but one look into Felipe's dark eyes had been all the reassurance she'd needed. He hadn't needed to spell it out, his eyes had told her everything she needed to know. He wouldn't let anything happen to her.

Once they'd made the brief walk from the car to the plane without incident, she'd been able to breathe. If they'd wanted to take her, they'd had their chance.

It was the money they were after. The money she'd foolishly agreed to bring *in cash* into Caballeros.

So, no, it wasn't fear currently gripping her. It was guilt, and mingled with it a strange form of exhilaration, an awareness of her blood pulsing through her veins. She'd never been so aware of being *alive*, of the sun's rays beaming onto her skin, of the soft material of her dress caressing her body, of the sweet scent of the air filling her lungs, all the small things she took for granted in her daily life sharply in focus as if she were experiencing them for the first time.

The closest she had come to this feeling before had been two nights ago in Felipe's arms.

She followed him through the hotel, marvelling at the strength of his frame, noticed again the slight limp, the only imperfection she could find on this magnificent man whose arms she longed to be in once more.

When they reached their suites, she opened her mouth to thank him and to apologise—again—for all the trouble her actions had brought on them.

Before she could speak, though, Felipe said,

'Come into mine for a minute while I get my stuff together.'

'Why? Are we changing hotels?'

'I'm changing rooms.' His features darkened. 'I'm moving into your suite. Until we trace those men and know who they're working for and what their intentions are, you're not to be alone.'

Far from sharing the thrill that raced through her at the thought of them sharing a suite, he had the face of a man tasked with guarding a hungry Venus flytrap.

She tailed him into his suite, a mirror image of her own, and took a seat on the sofa, watching as he pulled a large khaki kitbag from a cupboard and put it on the bed. He then walked into his dressing room and returned with an armful of clothes.

'Do you normally do sleepovers?' she asked, trying to lighten the atmosphere.

She was rewarded with a biting glare. 'This isn't a joke.'

'I know.'

'Then don't act as if it is.'

'What do you want me to do? Cower in a corner? Hide under a bed? It's obvious that they're after the money. All they're going to do is watch us until they know the cash is here… When is the money due?'

'Saturday. And it's obvious, is it? I thought you were training to be a lawyer. There's no clear evidence for a scenario so we're going to act as if any scenario is a possibility.'

'If it's me they want then they would have tried to take me already.'

'How do you know that?' he said through gritted teeth.

'An educated guess.'

'But still a guess.'

But she wasn't saying anything Felipe hadn't already thought. Whoever these men were, they'd had the opportunity to make a grab for her if it was indeed Francesca they wanted. These were cautious people he was dealing with, not hotheaded druggies. Stupid too. Parking just feet away from their Cessna and waiting for three hours without attempting to give themselves a cover story was the height of stupidity, and stupid people were the most dangerous.

His gut agreed with Francesca that they were after the money.

He could stay in his own suite in good conscience, content that she was safe in hers.

But he couldn't take the risk. Not with her. Just thinking it was enough for him to break out in a cold sweat.

What if his gut instinct born from almost two decades of risk assessments in dangerous situations was wrong?

This was why one didn't mix business with pleasure, he thought grimly, storming into the bathroom to get his toiletries. It clouded judgement. It made one doubt oneself.

Like it or not, his attraction to Francesca and the weight in his chest from being around her was accelerating. All his senses were attuned as if she were a magnet they were straining towards.

It was a fight to contain it. To protect her effectively he needed his head clear, a task made harder by the way she kept looking at him. If he could tune her out he would be fine. But he already knew tuning Francesca Pellegrini out was near on impossible.

One night alone in a suite with her he could handle. Any longer than that…

'I'm taking you back to Pisa in the morning,' he told her as he placed his toiletry bag with the rest of his kit, bracing himself for the furious protest that was bound to follow.

'No way,' she snapped, her nonchalance gone in an instant, just as he'd expected.

'It's too dangerous for you here. Pisa is safe. If I could take you back now I would but the quickest I can get a jet here is for early tomorrow morning and there's no commercial flights leaving any sooner. We'll leave first thing.'

'I'm not abandoning the project. No way.'

'You won't be abandoning it.' He would not allow her to set foot in that country again. 'You've got the agreement for the sale and met with the government's health representative. I'll get the cash to the Governor. Everything else can be handled by Daniele—he's the one who'll be getting the hospital built.'

'I'm going to the Governor's party,' she told him obstinately. 'If I don't attend he will see it as an insult and withdraw his permission and the hospital will never be built.'

Felipe swore loudly.

Damn it, she was right.

He thought quickly. The party was four days away. Plenty of time to draw up effective plans to protect both Francesca and the money.

'I'll fly you back for the party,' he said with a curt nod. 'But we leave here first thing in the morning. You'll be a sitting target if you stay. I'm taking you home where you'll be safe and I will have no further argument about it. When I bring you back, you will have nothing to do with the handover of the money. You will do exactly as you're told.'

He zipped his kitbag with more force than necessary and waited for another onslaught.

He knew he sounded like a tyrant but didn't care. The cold fear he'd experienced when he'd recognised that car had been like nothing he'd ever felt before, not even when he'd realised too late he'd led his men into a trap.

But no explosion came.

When he next looked at her, Francesca's legs were crossed, her fingers laced together, a thoughtful expression on her beautiful face as she studied him. Then her lips curved into a smile and she said, 'Does this mean we get to share a nightcap now?'

CHAPTER EIGHT

'I'M HUNGRY.'

A whole hour they'd been in her suite. A whole hour in which Felipe had ignored her existence, setting himself up with his laptop on the bureau in the corner.

For her part, Francesca had sat herself on the huge bed and watched him as studiously as he'd ignored her.

She could sense his awareness of her. It was in his every move, as strong as her awareness of him. The only difference was his resolve to pretend it didn't exist. His ridiculous rule of no *relations* with the client meant he was determined to fight it.

He regarded her as his responsibility and was doing everything in his power to keep her in the box he'd cast her in.

Well, she was determined to do everything in *her* power to pull herself out of that same box.

'I'm hungry,' she repeated.

He didn't look up from his laptop. 'You're always hungry. Order room service.'

'I had room service last night. It's only seven o'clock. If I spend another evening stuck in here, I'll get cabin fever. I'm going to get something to eat—are you coming with me?'

Now his eyes darted to hers and narrowed.

'I've agreed to go home in the morning,' she said sweetly, 'and I understand why you feel I need your full protection tonight. But I'm not going to be a prisoner in this suite. If you don't want to eat with me, call one of your men stationed around the hotel to join me instead.' She knew he would never go for that. She also knew that trying to draw him into conversation while in her suite would be akin to drawing blood from a stone. Without a laptop to hide behind he would be forced to talk to her.

Fury mounted in his returning glare but Francesca kept her gaze steady.

Then his glare turned into a look that could solidify gel. 'We eat, we come back. No drinking and no dancing. Is that understood?'

'Why don't you write it on a piece of paper so I don't forget? I'll sign it for you if you like.'

'Don't tempt me,' he growled.

'I'm doing my very best there.' She rose to her feet. 'I'm going to take a shower and make myself look beautiful before we leave. Is that okay with you, my lord and master?'

Certain he was cursing her in Spanish under his breath, Francesca sauntered to the bathroom.

Felipe waited for the click of the bathroom door's lock. When it didn't come he swore again. She'd deliberately left it unlocked.

He rubbed a knuckle to his forehead, trying not to think about what was going on behind the unlocked door.

Making herself look beautiful? It wasn't possible for Francesca to be more desirable than she already was.

The sound of the shower running came through the walls.

Do not think of her naked.

An email pinged into his inbox and he seized on the distraction; a recce report by a team of his men in North Africa in preparation for a business trip by the head of an American petroleum company.

He'd almost finished writing his reply when the bathroom door opened.

He looked up before he could stop himself.

Dios, Francesca had only a towel around herself.

'Don't mind me,' she said demurely, brushing past him and leaving a cloud of fruity scent in her wake, 'I'm just going to get changed.'

Gritting his teeth to counteract his thickening blood, he looked again at the email he was replying to.

She might as well have fired a bullet into his brain his concentration was so shot.

He blinked to refocus but, even when she disappeared into her dressing room, all he could see were bare slender arms and long black hair that, when wet, fell all the way to the base of her spine, almost touching the curvaceous bottom the white towel hugged so beautifully.

He knuckled his forehead and swore violently. She was taunting him. Tempting him. It was in her every look, her every movement.

The vows he'd made to himself in recent days were tested to the limit when she emerged some time later.

She'd changed into a Chinese-style red dress that was perfectly modest, not displaying any unnecessary flesh, falling to a decent length just above the knees, but…it clung to her every softly rounded curve…

And then he noticed she'd put make-up on. Not a huge amount but enough to make her light brown eyes even more seductive than they already were and her lips even more kissable. She'd blow-dried her hair and it hung like a silk sheet. On her feet were high black strappy sandals.

'Did you want to take a shower before we go?' she asked, appraising him with one of the gleams that fired straight into his groin.

He slammed the lid of his laptop down. 'Let's get this over with.'

Francesca swirled the white wine in her glass and watched Felipe study his menu.

He'd looked at her only once since they'd sat down, a piercing glare when she'd ordered her wine. She'd given an unrepentant shrug in return.

They were in one of the hotel's outdoor restaurants on a patio area that encircled a large swimming pool aglow with soft lighting.

Her intention had been to get Felipe out of the suite and get him talking. Whenever they'd had a proper conversation together they'd proved things could be harmonious between them. She wanted to find that harmony again.

She knew he desired her but what good was that when he fought it every step of the way? She wanted him to desire her company as well, to see her as herself. Francesca. Not Pieta's little sister. Not Daniele's little sister. Not the foolish client who'd agreed to a bribe because she hadn't been thinking straight and who needed saving from herself as well as the bad guys, whoever they were.

She waited until their order had been taken before asking, 'Where are you going when this job's done with?'

'Back to the Middle East.'

'You're not going home for a few days or anything?'

'Why do you want to know?'

'I'm making conversation. Annoying, I know, but one of us has to make the effort.'

Felipe tore his gaze from the distance he'd fixed on to look at her.

She tilted her head, her features softening. 'Please, Felipe, can't we just have a normal conversation like normal people?'

He smothered a sigh. It was far easier for him

to ignore the tightening of his loins that occurred just by being around her if he didn't have to listen to the husky voice that stroked his skin like a caress and stare into the beguiling eyes that had the power to hypnotise him.

Her request wasn't unreasonable.

He was the one being unreasonable.

She couldn't help it that every look made the yearning to touch her grow and his self-loathing ratchet up another notch.

'Do you still live in Spain?' she probed, taking his silence for assent.

'No.'

'Where do you live then?'

'Nowhere.'

'Nowhere?'

'Nowhere,' he confirmed. 'I have no home. I am of no fixed abode.'

'But…' She smoothed a long strand of hair behind her ear. A teardrop diamond earring winked at him. 'Where do you call home?'

He shrugged. 'Wherever I happen to be. I have a bedroom on my plane. Hotels are easy to come by. Everything I own is easily transported and as easily stored.'

She rocked forward slowly, a crease in her forehead. 'Where do your letters go? Bills? Bank statements? You have to have an address to have a bank account.'

'Not all banks require it if you know where to ask. My business isn't a typical one. My work is my life. It has been since I joined the army.'

She pulled a face. 'Yes, I get that. You're a macho man who runs around the world protecting the weak and helpless.'

A laugh crept up his throat. 'The majority of the people I protect are far from weak. It's generally business people, government officials and aid agencies. People who go to war zones and countries with high crime rates where they know they're going to be a target. My job is to let them do their jobs in safety.'

'Why does that stop you having a home of your own? Everyone needs a home.'

He shook his head. This was why he would have preferred to stay in the suite. There, he would have been able to work on his laptop, catch up on reports from his staff around the world, issue orders and directives, and ignore Francesca while ensuring her absolute safety. Here, there was nothing to do but talk while they waited for their food to be cooked and as he'd learned the other night in the hotel's main restaurant and their late-night conversation the night before, he enjoyed talking to Francesca far more than was good for him.

When they talked she became more than the alluring woman who made his blood thicken to look at her. She became flesh and blood.

The sooner this meal was finished the better.

'What about family?' she asked, oblivious to his wish—his *need*—for her silence. 'Do you see much of them?'

'No.'

'But you do have family?'

Felipe sighed. She didn't know when to give up. If Francesca made it to the bar she would be an excellent cross-examiner. 'I have a mother, grandparents, aunts, uncles, cousins. Yes. Family.'

'Do you see much of them?'

'No.'

'Why not?'

'I'm too busy.'

'Too busy to see your own mother?'

'I visit her whenever I can. The rest I was never close to so it's no loss.'

'No siblings?'

'I'm an only child.'

'Spoilt?'

He laughed harshly. Chance would have been a fine thing. 'No.'

'A father?'

'He died five years ago.'

The inquisitiveness on her features softened. 'I'm sorry. I lost my father last year. It's hard, I know.'

'It wasn't much of a loss. I hardly knew him.'

Seeing her open her mouth to ask another question, he leaned forward. 'My mother raised me as a single parent. They were married but my father was rarely there and rarely gave her money. She worked so many different jobs to put a roof over my head and food on the table that she was hardly there either, but she wasn't absent by choice as my father was. She didn't have the time or money to take me to Madrid to visit her family. We lived in Alicante, hundreds of miles from them. If my father hadn't been such a selfish chancer our lives would have been very different so, no, I didn't find his death hard. I went to his funeral out of respect but I am not going to pretend I grieved for him. I barely knew the man.'

His father had been unsuited to family life, a

man always on the road searching for the next big thing, which had never turned into anything, but that next big thing had always been more important to him than his wife and child.

So unimportant was his father to his life that he rarely thought about him, never mind talked about him, but with Francesca seemingly keen to interrogate him about his life, it was simpler to give her the full impartial facts and be done with it.

'That must have been hard for you. And your mamma,' she said, her eyes full of sympathy.

Thankfully their food was brought over to them by the cheerful waitress, T-bone steak for him and seared tuna pasta salad for Francesca.

She dived into hers and for a while he thought he'd escaped further interrogation.

Wrong.

'How often do you see your mother?'

'I try and visit over Christmas and for her birthday.'

'Is that it? Two visits a year?'

He took a large bite of his steak and ignored the implied rebuke. He didn't need to justify himself to her.

'If I only saw my mother twice a year she'd kill

me,' Francesca mused. 'She thinks I live too far from her as it is and I'm only a twenty-minute walk away.'

'You're her daughter. It's a different relationship.'

'Tell that to my brothers,' she said with a roll of her eyes that immediately dimmed, the vibrancy in them muting.

With a pang, he knew she was thinking of Pieta.

'Pieta was a good son to her,' she said quietly. 'He travelled all around the world but always remembered to call her every night. Daniele's the opposite—I'm always annoying him by sending reminders for him to call. She worries about us. Pieta's death has devastated her.'

'You're a close family,' he observed.

She nodded. 'I've been very lucky.'

Lucky until the brother she'd adored had been so tragically killed.

'Your life and background are very different from mine.'

'My life and background are different from most peoples. But, then, everyone's is. None of us are the same. We all have our worries.'

'You grew up rich and with a loving family. What worries did you have?'

'Me, personally? None that were serious. I was lucky and privileged but I know I'm one of the fortunate ones and it's why I want to go into human rights law.'

'You want to spread some of your good luck?'

'You may mock me but I'm serious. I could have settled down with a husband and babies by now but I want my life to mean something.'

He could only guess how hard she'd had to work to prove herself. He knew how old money worked—he'd protected enough of the people who lived in that world to know it was still male dominated. It couldn't have been easy for her to go against her family's expectations and wishes.

'You could run Pieta's foundation.'

Her pretty brow rose. 'Are you mocking me again?'

'Not at all. You were the consummate professional today. Pieta would have been proud of you.'

Her face flushed with pleasure. 'You think?'

'I'm sure of it, and I'm sure Alberto will be back at work soon. He could help and guide you. And keep you out of trouble,' he couldn't resist adding.

She half grinned and half scowled then shrugged

ruefully. 'It isn't for me. I want to get the hospital on Caballeros built for Pieta's memory but his philanthropy isn't the route I want to go. That was his and once things have settled we'll work as a family to make sure the foundation continues, but it won't be me running it. Maybe Natasha will.'

She fell silent after that, eating her food quietly, her thoughts obviously thousands of miles away with her family.

He watched her carefully. Underneath the front she put on she was grieving. He'd caught snatches of it during their time together, moments when she'd be talking to someone and, just like that, her eyes would lose their focus and her brow crease as if in confusion. And then, just as quickly, she would pull herself together and snap her focus back to the person before her.

She did it now. 'When was the last time you spoke to your mother?'

He could laugh at her single-mindedness. 'A couple of months ago.' At her exaggerated incredulity, he felt compelled to add, 'We've never been close in the way you are with your mother. Her whole life revolved around me and making sure all my needs were met but to get that she had to work fifteen hour days. I hardly knew her.' He hardly knew her now.

He took a long breath.

He really needed a beer.

Felipe raised his palm before she could ask anything else and said, 'It was a long time ago. I haven't lived with her for almost twenty years. We respect each other but she's not like your mother. She's not the clinging sort.'

'My mother doesn't cling,' she said defensively, then covered her mouth to hide a snort of laughter. 'Yes, she does cling. But I don't mind. I like it.'

'And I like the relationship my mother and I have. It suits us both.'

She cast him with a look of pure disbelief then shrugged as if to say it was a point she couldn't bother arguing. 'Is her life easier now?'

'Much easier. I've bought her a house and a car, I send her regular money. She doesn't need to work. She has friends and goes on dates. She has a life now, which she never had before.'

That perked her up. 'You bought her a house?'

He groaned, sensing a new thread of his life for her to delve into. 'Can we not talk of something else?'

'Okay, tell me why you joined the army.'

'Because I was turning into a juvenile delinquent with no parental authority and no hope of getting a decent job because there was no one there to make sure I attended school.'

'How long were you in the army for?'

'Eight years in all.' And they had been the best years of his life. The camaraderie, the companionship…after a childhood spent alone the army had given him the family he'd always craved. In Sergio he'd found the brother he'd always longed for.

How could the woman sitting opposite him understand any of this? Her family was as close as a family could be. She'd never eaten her childhood meals alone with only the television for company. She'd never *been* alone. She'd never wanted for anything, not materially or emotionally. It had all been handed to her on a plate.

So why was he fighting his own tongue from spilling the rest of it out to her?

It was those eyes, the way they smouldered and hung on to his every answer.

Every time he stared into those honest eyes a pulse would flow through him. He'd scrubbed his hands over and over but could still feel the softness of her skin and the silkiness of her hair on his fingers as if they'd marked him. When she'd been standing with Eva, the charity worker, he'd distinguished Francesca's scent without even thinking about it.

He knew her *scent.*

During their conversation, without him realising how, they'd both cleared their plates.

It was time to bring to a close this ordeal he'd enjoyed far too much.

He got to his feet. 'We can go back to the suite now.'

She stared up at him with such hurt at his brusqueness that he felt much as he would have if he'd kicked a puppy. Like a heel.

Instead of obeying, she folded her arms, the obstinate look he was becoming accustomed to setting on her jaw. But her eyes were knowing as she said, 'I think I'll stay for dessert.'

CHAPTER NINE

'YOU'RE WELCOME TO share my bed,' Francesca said brightly as Felipe made a bed on the floor for himself close to the door, using the duvet, spare sheets and pillows from his suite.

He didn't look at her. He'd returned to ignoring her and speaking in monosyllabic grunts ever since she'd insisted on staying for dessert.

Her insistence on staying had been a deliberate kick-back. Felipe had relaxed over their meal and opened up to her, not by much but enough for her chest to lighten and hope to spring free. A proper conversation between two adults enjoying each other's company. There were times he'd looked at her as if he wanted to eat her, the desire in his eyes vivid… But then he'd withdrawn as quickly as if he'd pulled the trigger on a gun.

Now he was back to looking at her as if he'd like to chuck her in the sea.

'Why don't you stop talking and get ready

for bed?' he growled. 'Tomorrow's going to be a long day.'

'I'm not tired.'

'Read a book.'

She wished she knew what it would take to pull his barriers down long enough for him to forget his reasons for resisting and simply treat her as a woman. That's all she wanted.

'I'll put my nightclothes on in the bathroom, shall I?'

'*Yes*!'

'Okay. I won't be long. Try not to miss me.'

It didn't take long for her to change into the over-sized T-shirt she slept in, wash her face and brush her teeth, all the while wondering if she had the courage to go for full-scale seduction.

She could hardly believe she was having these thoughts.

Pieta's death had brought home how short and fickle life could be. The dangers of Caballeros had reinforced that notion. All those years she'd spent studying, any thought of a romantic life pushed aside so as not to distract her from her dreams… It had stopped her *feeling* life rather than just going through the motions of living it.

Felipe was nothing like the rich, boring, single

men her parents had brought in a steady trickle to the family home before she'd escaped to university, hoping their darling daughter would snare one of them and marry into luxury and be doted on. The only similarity he had with them was that he was fabulously rich.

Francesca hadn't wanted to be doted on. Her mother had married young and was content to live the life of a social butterfly where the biggest daily problem would be matching her nail varnish with her outfit. Francesca had wanted so much more. She had wanted to be like her brothers and cousin Matteo. They were also expected to settle down and breed but at a much older age. They were expected to have fantastic careers first, whereas she'd been expected to adorn her husband's fantastic career. She hadn't wanted to adorn or be beholden to a man. She'd wanted a fantastic career of her own and had known from a very young age that the only way to get it was by studying as hard as she could to get the highest possible grades so her parents had no choice but to take her and her aspirations seriously.

She had succeeded. There had been many fights and many tears but eventually they had accepted her wishes. That hadn't stopped them parading eligible rich men in front of her but the tone had changed; become hope rather than expectation.

If she continued working hard, in two years she would sit her bar exams and qualify as a lawyer, then spend a few more years establishing herself in the career she'd devoted her life to achieving. Only then would she think of making a marriage, safe in the knowledge that, whoever she chose, her hard-won independence would not be compromised and the marriage would be conducted as equals.

That had been the plan.

What she hadn't expected was this awakening, this heady desire for a man that no amount of logic could explain.

She didn't want to explain it. She wanted to explore it, to reach out and touch it and experience these wonderful feelings that had soaked into her being, all of which were for Felipe.

He was not a man to dote on a woman. He was strong and protective but would never treat a woman as a pet.

And he didn't want a relationship either.

If anything were to happen between them it

would be nothing but a short, sweet affair that wouldn't compromise either of their chosen paths.

The problem, Francesca acknowledged ruefully, came with the *if*.

It would help if she knew how to seduce a man, let alone one so determined to keep her at arm's length. And wasn't seduction supposed to be conducted wearing sexy lingerie? She wore pretty underwear but nothing that could be considered sexy or lingerie.

All she had was herself.

When she walked back into the suite she found Felipe kneeling by his huge khaki kitbag.

He looked at her briefly then closed his eyes and muttered something under his breath before pulling out his washbag. 'I'm going to take a shower.'

A moment later came the telling click of the bathroom lock.

Taking a deep breath, Francesca turned all the lights off apart from her bedside one, giving the room a soft seductive quality. Then she got onto the huge bed and arranged herself into what she hoped was a seductive pose. Instead of making her feel wanton it made her feel like a fool so she tried a different pose. That made her feel a bigger fool. After trying a variety of others she settled for sitting with her legs stretched out and hooked at the ankles, her head resting on the headboard.

Felipe spent so long in the bathroom that doubts began to crowd her. Did she have his feelings for her all wrong?

Were those times when she looked in his eyes and saw pained desire burning back at her nothing but creations of her own tortured mind, like a child desperate to see Father Christmas swearing blind they saw him flying his reindeer past their bedroom window? Nothing but a hopeful, overactive imagination?

She sensed when he was ready to leave his sanctuary and swallowed, placing a hand to her rapidly beating heart.

The bathroom door opened. Their eyes met.

He held her gaze a beat too long then broke it, striding past her to the nest he'd made by her door.

She watched his every step with her heart in her mouth.

Francesca had seen Felipe with nothing but tight swim shorts on at the swimming pool but she had been some distance away. Up close his magnificence was stark enough to steal her breath and set her already ragged pulses soaring. Up close there was no escaping the bulge in the snug black boxers he wore.

Even a straight man would do a double take at him.

A silvery mark on his right calf caught her eye, pulling her out of the trance she'd slipped into. 'What happened to your leg?'

'Gunshot,' he answered gruffly.

His answer had her pressing the switch behind her to turn the corner light on.

Her hand flew to her mouth.

It wasn't just a silvery mark; there was a hollowed out section of flesh around his shin bone that covered half his calf.

Thick icy sludge crawled up her spine and through her veins, freezing her from the inside out.

She could hardly get her vocal cords working to whisper, 'What happened to you?'

'The perils of army life.'

'You were shot in battle?'

'Something like that.'

Feeling faint, she took a long breath, unable to look away from the ugly wound that made her heart hurt.

Felipe was a military man. She'd known that before she'd met him. It was his career in the army, including his time in the Special Forces, that made him so effective at what he did, that had given him the solid foundations to build the hugely successful enterprise he had now.

Yet whenever she thought about the armed forces—admittedly, before she'd met Felipe that had been rarely—she'd imagined it to be like those computer games she'd been banned from watching Daniele play when he'd been younger and she much younger still but, of course, had sneakily peeked in on. She hadn't seriously thought about what it must be like to be in a real war, to have people firing at you not for fun but because they wanted to kill you.

Someone had shot Felipe with the intention of killing him.

He must have noticed her horror for his expression hardened. 'I apologise if my wound disgusts you.'

'No.' She shook her head, trying to clear it, trying to refocus her eyes. 'Don't think that. *I* don't think that. Felipe…' She shook her head some more.

Now the limp she'd often noticed made sense.

As if to distract her attention from his wound, Felipe slid into the makeshift bed he'd made for himself on the floor, thumped the top pillow and lay on his back, gazing at the ceiling with his arm crooked above his head.

Francesca turned the corner light off so the only illumination in the suite came from her bedside light.

She felt chilled to her core. If whoever had shot at him had had a better aim the vital, intense man who lay in a nest of bedding at her door would not be here. He would be gone from this earth like Pieta, nothing but a memory. But not a memory to her because she never would have met him.

She remembered Daniele—or was it Matteo?—saying Felipe had been discharged from the army on medical grounds.

'Was that the reason you left the army?'

Even with the limited light she saw his grimace. 'Yes. The wound meant I was no longer an effective soldier. It's standard procedure. It wasn't personal.'

'Would you have stayed if you could?'

'I would have stayed for as long as they'd had me. I loved the life.'

'You loved going into war zones?'

He let out a low rumble of laughter. 'Believe it or not, yes. I thrived on the danger. We all did. I loved everything about army life. Passing selection for the Special Forces was the best day of my life. Receiving my discharge was the worst.'

Felipe had known as soon as the bullet had hit him that it was the end of his army career and the end of everything he'd held dear. The bullet had splintered in his leg, shrapnel lodging in the bones. There had been talk of amputation.

The long months spent in rehabilitation, working into a sweat just to walk again, dealing with the pain of his wound and the darkness of what he'd lost…it had all brought home to him that he was meant to be alone.

When it was just you in the world the only threat of pain was the physical kind. He'd proven he could deal with that. Physical pain was mind over matter. Determination. It hurt but didn't leave you bereft and empty inside.

For once Francesca was silent. He knew it wouldn't be for long. He was right.

'Is that why you went into protection? So you could still get the adrenaline buzz?'

'The world is full of dangers and people still need to visit those danger zones. I knew I could provide the protection they needed and that there were many other soldiers like me who were fit and ready for the next challenge.' But not Sergio. The first bullet that had hit him had gone straight into his heart.

'Do you get the same fulfilment you got from the army?'

'It's a different kind of fulfilment.' Even though he'd thrown all his energy into it, he could never have guessed how successful his business would be. He had more money than he could spend in a thousand lifetimes, was on the speed dial of the world's most powerful people, but knew that given the choice of swapping his riches for a return to his army days he would discard his worldly goods without a second thought.

'Don't you ever wish for a normal life?' she whispered in the silence.

'What's your definition of a normal life?'

'One that's not completely nomadic.'

'No.' Yet as he spoke his rebuttal he found his mind meandering for the first time ever to a real home with an ebony-haired beauty…

He pushed the thought away. A normal, regular life was not for him.

'That's enough talk. We've an early start. Get some sleep.'

'But—'

'I mean it. No more conversation.'

But he knew the chances of his getting any sleep were slim, not when he was certain that beneath her oversized T-shirt Francesca lay naked.

He closed his eyes and willed his mind not to think of her naked.

Dios, this was torture. He ached to join her in that bed.

In his head he counted out the reasons why he needed to stay exactly where he was.

One. She was his client.

Two. She was grieving.

'It's not even ten o'clock. I'm not tired. I never go to bed this early.'

Just the sound of her voice was enough to make Felipe's loins tighten.

'Read your book,' he said through gritted teeth.

There was another long period of silence but he sensed a shift in the atmosphere, a change in her mood.

'"*Read your book, stop talking, go to sleep*",' she mimicked suddenly. 'It's one step forward and two steps back with you, isn't it? One minute you're opening up and talking to me like a normal human being, the next you act like you're trying to forget my existence. Do you treat all your clients like this?'

He smothered a groan at the hurt echoing in her voice. 'Like what?'

'Like they're an encumbrance to be endured. Sometimes it feels that you don't even like me.'

He clenched his jaw. What did she want him to say? Mere *liking* had nothing to do with his feelings for her.

'It's different with my other clients.' He'd never struggled with professional detachment before. He'd never wanted to rip any of their clothes off.

'So it's true!' As quick as a flash she threw her covers off and jumped off the bed. 'You don't like me. I thought it was the attraction between us you hated.' She stormed into her dressing room and slammed her hand against the switch, bathing the room in fresh light. 'I didn't realise the problem was that you actively dislike *me*.'

'I *don't*...' But his words fell from his lips when she pulled her T-shirt off. Even with the distance between them, he could see her clearly, from the divine weighty breasts with their dark aureoles to the soft womanly hair between her legs.

Oh, dear heaven…

Francesca was heaven. A taste of paradise wrapped up in beautiful, womanly form.

But then she grabbed the dress she'd been wearing earlier and he understood what she was doing.

Springing to his feet, he strode over and blocked the doorway of her dressing room. 'Where do you think you're going?'

'For a drink. Anywhere away from you.'

Fire blazed from her eyes, her whole body vibrating with anger. And, *Dios*, no matter how hard he tried he couldn't stop his eyes from devouring her, naked before him, not an ounce of embarrassment in her returning fury.

Then she tilted her chin and pulled the dress over her head. The delectable curves disappeared as she smoothed the dress down and tugged her trapped hair free. As it tumbled down her back he couldn't help but fantasise what it would feel like to have that hair tumble over *him* in all its silken glory.

'Get out of my way,' she said coldly.

'No.'

Slowly, her fiery gaze holding his, she stepped to him. When she was close enough for his senses to be hit with her scent, she put her wrists together and held them out to him. 'If you're intending to treat me as a prisoner you might as well tie me up because that's the only way you're going to stop me leaving this room.'

Electricity shot between them, so real he could almost hear the crackle. It heated him too, tiny jolts bouncing on his skin, his heart thrumming…

His hand rose by its own volition, his fingers stretching towards her.

A throb of need burst through him, so powerful he had to dig his feet into the floor to stop from hauling her into his arms.

'You are not leaving this suite.' His speech was long, drawn out, ragged.

'I'm not staying with someone who can barely look at me and gets irritated every time I open my mouth.'

Without him knowing how it happened, his fingers closed around the delicate wrists. A moment later he'd pulled her to him so their bodies were flush, her breasts pressed against his chest.

'I don't dislike you,' he ground out, gazing down at the spitting eyes, the luminous skin, the lips that begged to be kissed… 'Don't you see that? I like you *too much*.'

For long, long moments they did nothing but stare at each other until the anger that blazed so brightly in her eyes softened to blaze with something that struck straight into his loins.

Francesca stared helplessly at the man who had her in a grip so tight she could never break free yet which elicited not the slightest amount of pain.

The humiliation that had washed over her like a cold shower at the realisation she'd been longing for a man who hated her vanished as awareness filled her in its stead, awareness of his heat, of being held against this dangerously masculine man her body craved.

She had no conscious reckoning of the change in him, of how the fury deepened into something so dark and molten her chest filled, of the deepening of his breaths as he continued to gaze down at her…

'I can't hear your voice without becoming aroused,' he said, his voice low, pained. 'I can't look at you without wanting to kiss you. I can't breathe your scent without wanting to possess you. Wanting you like this is torture.'

'Then stop fighting it,' she whispered.

Later she would have no conscious remembrance of the moment his lips moulded onto hers. It was like a beast that lived inside them both suddenly became unleashed.

There was nothing gentle about his kiss or her response to it. It burned her, ravaged her. All her nerve endings exploded and leapt onto him. The hand that had been holding her wrists was now wrapped tightly around her waist, her arms now looped tightly around his neck, kissing as if they needed the other for air, lips parted, devouring each other.

She grabbed at the back of his head and raked her fingers through his hair, nuzzling, kissing, nipping, her senses filling with his very essence, all the hunger she had for him soaring free.

His arousal pressed hard and huge against her belly, his hands roamed her contours, kneading, fingers biting. The evidence of his desire for her was dizzying and heightened her own. The desire she'd experienced during the alcohol-induced fumble that had gone further than either of them had expected had been like a carnal dream but this…sober…everything felt gloriously, dizzily heightened and *urgent*, no slow sensual build-up, her body craving nothing less than full possession.

He broke the kiss to place his hands at her waist and lift her into the air like a ballet dancer lifting his partner. Her hair fell onto his shoulders and he turned his face to breathe the scent of it in. '*Dios*, I want you,' he muttered raggedly.

Without another word said he sat her on the edge of the bed and pressed her down so he lay on top of her, crushing her, his heart drumming strongly enough for her to feel it against her own hammering heart. Their lips entwined in another deep, hungry kiss and he ran a hand up her thigh to take the hem of her dress and raise it to her waist.

Needing to touch him, she ran her fingers down his back and revelled in the smoothness of his skin, the muscles that bunched beneath her touch, then traced lower to the tight buttocks. Grasping frantically, she found the waistband of his boxers and tugged at them. Felipe's hand covered hers and together they shifted them down his hips, allowing his erection to spring free.

Her eyes flew open to feel the weight of his excitement against her inner thigh, a deep throb pulsing through her to know this was for her. Her own arousal had melted into a mass of heat and dampness, all concentrating in the one area he was so close to taking possession of.

Francesca had never dreamt she was capable of such wanton, reckless carnality, that her flesh could feel like a living being, that desire could beat like a drum with a rhythm felt in her every pore.

This, she thought dreamily… *This*…

Instinct had her raising her thighs and wrapping her legs around Felipe's waist, urging him on, her body speaking the language she had never learned.

The tip of his erection found where it needed to be with no guidance from either of them and in one driving thrust he was inside her.

It happened so quickly that it took a few beats for her brain to register the sharp pain and when it did register, the gasp of relief at his possession that had flown from her mouth turned into a gasp of shock and stilled on her lips.

Felipe froze.

The heady urgency of his desire deflated like a punctured balloon. He gazed down in horror at Francesca's whitening face.

It wasn't possible...

His head pounded loudly, bells clanging, sirens wailing.

It wasn't possible.

With as great a care as he could manage, he withdrew from her and swung his legs over to rest on the floor then grabbed the back of his neck and dug his fingers into it.

The beat of his heart was out of time.

She didn't move.

He didn't move.

For the longest time he sat on the bed staring incomprehensibly at the thick carpet while she lay on the bed gazing mutely at the ceiling.

He wanted to be sick. There was movement beside him as Francesca slowly sat up.

A trembling finger was placed lightly on his shoulder.

'Felipe…'

Slowly he raised his head and caught sight of himself in the mirror on the wall.

The reflection gazing back was a man he didn't recognise.

He didn't think he would ever recognise himself again.

CHAPTER TEN

WHEN HIS THROAT had loosened enough so he could breathe, Felipe got to his feet and put his boxers on. Only then did he turn to the hunched figure in the centre of the bed. She still had her dress on.

Francesca's eyes were huge but when he met them he saw they were filled with defiance as well as misery.

With a sigh, he sank back onto the edge of the bed and buried his face in his hands. 'You should have told me.'

Her voice was low but steady. 'If I'd told you, you would have stopped.'

'Damn right I would have stopped.' He swore loudly as he remembered something else that made the hairs on arms lift. 'We didn't even use protection.' Not that they'd needed it. It had been over almost as soon as it had begun.

'I'm on the Pill,' she mumbled.

'Are you?' he demanded. 'You're not just saying that?'

A quick shake of her head. 'I used to have terrible pains every month. The Pill helped.'

'Francesca… *Dios*…' He raised his head and met her gaze. 'What were you thinking?'

She didn't answer.

'Was it your intention to make me hate myself?'

She shook her head and blinked rapidly. If she cried, he thought there was every chance he would lose the plot completely.

How was it possible she'd been a virgin?

'For God's sake, will you say something? Tell me what's going on in that head of yours?'

'I thought you wanted me to shut up,' she whispered with a forlorn smile.

His hands clenched into fists and he swore loudly.

She screwed her eyes tight shut.

He fought to control his tone, to soften it. 'Francesca, please, tell me why you didn't think fit to inform me you were a virgin. Don't you understand how sick I am at myself for what just happened? My self-loathing would have been high enough but discovering that…' He threw his hands in the air. His affairs had always been conducted with experienced women who knew better than to expect anything from him. Did Francesca giving her virginity to him mean she wanted more? 'Why didn't you stop me?'

'Because I wanted it to happen,' she said so quietly he had to strain to hear.

'But *why*? There can never be anything between us, don't you understand that? Even when this is all over and you're no longer my client, you and I can never be.'

'Why? Because I'm too young for you?' Her voice shook. 'I'm twenty-three, not thirteen, old enough to marry, to vote, to drive, to work, to make mistakes and be judged old enough to know better.'

'No!' His voice rose as he lost the battle with his temper. 'I don't do relationships. I told you this. You were a twenty-three-year-old virgin for a reason, I assume because you were waiting for the right man or for marriage. I could never be that man!'

'I don't want you to be that man!' Francesca shouted back. Her shame and Felipe's anger had pushed her to breaking point. 'Stop making assumptions about me. I wasn't *saving* myself.

Haven't you listened to me? I've told you more than once I don't intend to settle down for years, not until I've set up my own law firm. I want a career first, thank you, and when I do marry it will be to someone who can treat me as his equal. You are *not* that man.'

'Then *why*?' He gripped the back of his head and breathed deeply. 'Please, explain it to me so I don't spend the rest of my life hating myself for taking advantage of your vulnerability. And do not deny that you're vulnerable, you buried the brother you loved only days ago and something like that does affect you even if you don't see it at the time.'

She dragged her fingers down her face and tried to control the violent trembling racking her body.

Whenever she'd imagined them together, and in the past few days it had seemed that was *all* she'd thought about, she'd blithely assumed he wouldn't notice she was a virgin and that she would have the wit to smother any pain because everyone said the pain only lasted a moment.

She'd known perfectly well he would reinforce the barrier he'd put between them if he knew she was a virgin and seeing his self-loathing horror at what they'd done made her feel more wretched and ashamed of herself than she had believed she could feel.

Had it been such a bad thing, keeping quiet about her virginity? It was her body. Wasn't she free to do with it as she wished?

Silence filled the room as she composed her thoughts and tried to compose herself, biting back the tears that were right there, waiting to be unleashed.

'I know Pieta's death's affected me,' she whispered. 'It's made me see how short life can be. I could get a terminal illness or get hit by a car or be the victim of a natural disaster... People die every day. You've walked the streets of Caballeros with me...you've been in battle, you must feel life's fragility.'

A tear leaked down her cheek. She wiped it away before continuing. 'I'm not trying to be morbid. Before Pieta died... I'm trying to make you understand what it was like. I knew from the time I could speak that I would never inherit anything and I remember my mamma stroking my hair when I was seven and saying what a pretty girl I was and how lucky I was that I would have my pick of rich husbands and always live a life of luxury. My looks and my family name were expected to be enough for me to have a great future but I remember feeling sick at the thought of it.

'Daniele wasn't going to inherit but he was expected to build a great life for himself—why should it be different for me because I was girl? Why should my future depend on what would, essentially, be the goodwill of a man I hadn't even met? Why should I be forced to beg for money to buy the clothes I need when I can earn it myself and control my own life? I think that was the moment I decided I would take my own path and prove that anything my brothers could do, I could do too, and do it better. I've spent my whole life working towards that. But I didn't live like a recluse. I partied and had fun but relationships… I saw how my friends were with their boyfriends and how their relationships consumed their lives and knew I couldn't afford that distraction.'

While she spoke, Felipe didn't say anything, listening with narrowed eyes without comment.

She met his gaze and tried to smile but instead found herself wiping away another tear. 'Until eleven days ago I never had the sense that it could all end at any moment. My father's death was awful but he'd been in his seventies and had been ill for years. In many ways the end was a relief for him. Pieta was only thirty-five, young, fit, recently married, a whole future to look forward to and it was all taken away in a moment by something as innocuous as fog. *Fog*!' She could laugh at the madness and cruelty of it.

To watch her father slowly disintegrate had been heart-breaking but his faculties, his sense of humour…they had all survived in him to the very end. They'd had time to prepare. Nothing could have prepared her or any of them for Pieta's death.

'All those people who died in the hurricane in Caballeros, they'd had futures and family too, people who loved them. If it could happen to Pieta and to them, then why not me?'

Felipe made to speak but she raised a hand to stop him.

'Whether I have days left to live or years or decades, I want to live it to be the best I can but I want to *feel* it too. You make me feel things I've never felt before. Good feelings. Scary feelings. But *real* feelings.' Feelings she'd ached to explore to see where they would take her because *what if she never felt them again*? 'Do you understand that?'

His dark eyes held hers as he gave a sharp inclination of his head.

'I don't know if it was this new awareness of life and its fragility that woke these feelings up or if it was just the catalyst…' She attempted a smile. 'No, I do know. If I'd met you under different circumstances I still would have wanted you. What I don't know is if I would have had acted on it. I don't expect anything from you or want anything more than this. Don't think you took advantage of me. I gave my body to you freely as a consenting woman, just as you gave yours freely to me as a consenting man.'

She tried to smile again but her chin wobbled too much for it to form. 'And that's it.'

As Felipe listened, his fury with both Francesca and himself slowly seeped from him.

Curled on the huge bed, she looked so intensely vulnerable that his heart ached.

His pulses hammering, he shifted closer to her and took her cold hands, which just a short time ago had been warm, and rubbed them gently between his own then pressed a kiss to them.

She attempted another shaky smile that made the ache in his heart expand.

'I hurt you, didn't I?' he said quietly.

She drew her lips in and nodded. 'That was my own fault. If you'd known…'

'If I'd known it was your first time I would have taken it slowly, not taken you like a rutting bull.'

She pulled a face. 'If you'd known it was my first time you wouldn't have taken me at all. That's why I didn't tell you.'

He laughed, his chest lightening at her wry quip.

'You're right, I have made many assumptions about you, *querida*,' he said, reaching out to stroke her pale cheek. 'It's the nature of my life. I work with men, the people I protect are normally men too.'

Women had always been on the periphery of his life, even his own mother, too busy working to feed him for him to learn any feminine secrets. Women were a mystery. He'd shared his bed with many of them through the years but had no clue as to how their minds worked. Francesca was the closest he'd come to understanding.

'Women have always seemed like a different

species to me,' he admitted ruefully. 'I accepted your family's description of you being a danger to yourself at face value, which I wouldn't have done if you'd been a man.'

'Maybe they were right,' she whispered.

He shook his head, knowing she was thinking back to her gung-ho response to the Governor's demand for a cash bribe. 'To begin with you were on the edge but you soon found the strength you needed. What I am trying to say in my clumsy way is that I've not been able to look past my initial assumptions and too busy fighting my attraction to you to see you as you really are.'

'How do you see me now?'

'As strong.' *And beautiful.* 'You're a fighter, *querida*.'

Another tear rolled down her cheek. She screwed her face up as he wiped it away with his thumb.

'Not very strong now,' she mumbled.

He leaned forward and cupped her face in his hands. 'I've seen men bigger than me cry. It's nothing to do with strength and nothing to be ashamed of.'

She sighed and nodded then seemed to gather herself together, her back straightening. 'I should put my nightshirt on.'

Her legs made a slight wobble as she padded to the dressing room and closed the door behind her, re-emerging moments later with her nightshirt on.

She stood in the doorway and tucked a stray lock of hair behind her ear. 'What happens now?'

His heart hurt to see her vulnerability. He couldn't turn his back on it, not yet.

'Now, *querida*, we get some sleep.' Sliding under the bedsheets, he opened his arms to her.

Tentatively she walked to him. When she climbed onto the bed he switched the bedside light off then gently laid her down so she was nestled against him.

Holding her tightly, he lay with her in silence, his mind still reeling from everything that had just happened, his loins still aching from unfulfilled desire.

Instead of acting on it, he did nothing more than stroke her hair and trace his fingers gently over the top of her back.

He'd never held a woman like this before. It was an intimacy he'd always steered away from.

He couldn't stay here holding her like this. Equally, he couldn't leave her. Not yet.

Only when Francesca's breathing had become

deep and regular, her limbs weighty on him, did he extricate himself and settle in his makeshift bed on the floor, attempting to calm his racing head and thrumming heart enough to find some sleep of his own.

Felipe opened his eyes, instantly alert to any sound.

The suite was in darkness. All was quiet. But something had woken him.

Then he heard it again, the sound that had roused him from his sleep. A whimper.

He threw his covers off and climbed onto the bed where he found Francesca curled in a ball, crying into her pillow.

'Querida?' Tentatively, he put a hand on her head.

She stilled at his touch. After a moment she turned her face and opened her eyes. 'Felipe?'

He smoothed damp hair from her wet face. 'What's the matter?'

Her face crumpled and tears fell down her cheeks, silvery in the shadowed darkness.

'A bad dream?'

She gave a jerky nod.

He scooped her up to pull her to him and wrapped his arms tightly around her.

'Hush,' he whispered, kissing the top of her head. 'It's over now.'

Clinging to him as if he were a life raft, she sobbed into his chest.

'It's over now,' he repeated, feeling as ineffectual as it was possible to feel.

He'd held fellow soldiers in his arms when they'd sobbed over a fallen comrade, but never had he held them and heard the cracks of his own heart.

If he had the power, he would snatch out the terror that had taken her into its hold and bury it for ever.

'It's over.'

Her hair brushed against his chin as she shook her head. 'It will never be over.'

He held her until the shudders ceased and the tears dried up, then got under the covers and lay beside her, still holding her to him.

'It will get better,' he whispered, stroking her hair. 'Not yet, not for a long time, but one day.'

'How?' she asked dully into his chest.

'I know loss. Grief has to come out. You've

been keeping yourself so busy during the day it's coming out at night.'

She was silent for a long moment before saying in a small voice, 'It's not grief. It's guilt.'

'Guilt over Pieta?'

She nodded.

'How can you feel guilt, *querida*? You weren't in the helicopter with him.'

There was another lengthy silence. When she eventually replied her voice was so low and muffled it was a struggle to hear clearly.

'When Mamma called me to tell me my brother had died, I thought she was talking about Daniele. He's always travelling by helicopter. I didn't realise it was Pieta until she asked me to go with her to tell Natasha.'

'Why would you feel guilty about that?'

'Because my first emotion when I realised it was Pieta was relief that it wasn't Daniele.'

Francesca waited for a reaction from him, a condemnation, however subtle.

His only response was to tighten his hold and rub his mouth into her hair.

'I haven't told anyone that,' she whispered. 'I tried to deny it to myself but he won't let me forget.'

'Who won't?'

'Pieta. He's haunting my dreams. He knows how I felt. He knows the truth and he won't let me forget it.'

'That's not possible,' he said gently, his breath warm against her skull. 'They say dreams are our subconscious talking to us and I know it to be true from my own experience. That's all it is.'

'My guilty conscience talking to me?' She swallowed back more tears.

'Yes. But you have nothing to feel guilty about.'

'I have everything to feel guilty about.'

'Did you wish Pieta dead?'

'*No*!' The idea was so horrific that she disentangled herself from his hold and sat up. 'No. Of course I didn't. He was my brother and I loved him.'

'And he knew that.' He took her hand and laced his fingers through hers. 'He was your hero.'

She smiled wistfully and squeezed his interlinked fingers. 'I did love him. I really did. But I was never close to him as I am to Daniele. He left home to go to university when I was six so I only have faint memories of living with him. He was this mythological being who would sweep into the family home at various times bearing thoughtful gifts. He would sit down with me and ask me questions and listen closely to all my answers. He encouraged me in everything I did. Truly, he was a brilliant big brother but…'

'But?' Felipe asked into the silence.

'He was detached. I never connected emotionally to him. Daniele's a lot older than me too but he was a *proper* brother. He teased me and tormented me, and I teased and tormented him back. When I went to university, he was always dropping in on a whim if he was in Pisa, taking me out in his newest car or jet or whatever expensive toy he'd recently brought. He took me shopping, brought me my first legal drink…'

'He was the fun one?' Felipe suggested.

'Yes. That. The fun one. That wasn't Pieta's fault. He was raised the eldest son, knowing the family's estate would pass to him, that keeping it intact for the next generation would be his responsibility. He was very serious. When I started working for him at his law firm I hoped we would get closer and I would see another side to him. I thought we would go out for lunch together and have after work drinks.'

'It didn't happen?'

'We never had the time. I only started my traineeship a few months ago and Pieta was rarely there as he was always travelling. I was put under the charge of one of his senior lawyers.'

She sighed and lay back down, resting her head next to his. All that time she'd thought she would have to finally get to know her oldest brother, all gone in an instant.

'Pieta was a hard man to get to know,' Felipe said quietly. 'I worked with him many times on his philanthropic missions. He was a good man and I enjoyed his company.'

'But?' she prompted, certain he wanted to say more.

He rolled onto his side to look at her, so close his nose brushed hers. 'He kept people at arm's length. I don't think there were many people he allowed to see his real self.'

'I wish things could have been different between us and that we'd been closer.'

'I know you do. Pieta was just a man doing the best he could with the hand he'd been dealt. I'm sure he didn't mean to shut you out.'

Francesca gazed at him, her chest feeling so much lighter yet, conversely, unbelievably full.

'Thank you,' she whispered.

'For what?'

'For listening and not judging.'

He kissed the tip of her nose.

She thought back to his earlier comment about the subconscious. 'What was it that gave you bad dreams?'

She caught the flash of pain in his eyes.

Palming his cheek, she stroked the soft beard. Tentatively, she probed, 'Is it from when you were shot?'

He covered her hand with his own. 'I lost my closest friend that day. I watched him die.'

'Oh, Felipe,' she breathed with a sympathy she felt right in the centre of her being.

'The Special Forces do many classified covert missions. This was one of them. The most I can tell you about it is that a group of Spanish executives were taken hostage in a North African country by a guerrilla group. My unit was flown in to rescue them. Our intelligence was faulty. We were told there were three hostage takers but there were eight of them. It was a bloodbath. We lost ten of the hostages and I lost three of my men. Good men. Sergio was shot first. He'd been by my side since our basic training days when we were green eighteen-year-olds. We took selection for the Special Forces together...we were as close as brothers. I was best man at his wedding. I was to be godfather to his child. I lost everything that day—my brother, my army family and the career I loved.'

Francesca, her heart in her mouth, stared into the dark eyes and wished with all her heart that she could find the words to take his pain away.

No wonder he understood her pain so much. He must have been battling his own nightmares for the past decade.

His overprotectiveness and desire to plan for each and every eventuality suddenly made perfect sense. Even the business he'd formed, protecting civilians, ensuring they were as safe as they could be, never leaving anything to chance. She would bet her career none of his clients had ever been taken hostage while under his protection.

It also made sense of his solitude. Here was a man who'd spent his childhood alone but in the army had found a place where he belonged, only to have it all ripped away from him in one disastrous mission.

This time she was the one to wrap her arms around him and hold him close so his head was nestled in the crook of her neck, his beard scratching her collarbone.

She swallowed a lump away and closed her eyes, trying to process how everything had turned on its head.

This closeness she felt with Felipe right now…

Did sex always lead to such emotional intimacy?

How did men find it so easy to conduct meaningless affairs? How could Daniele and Matteo hop from one bed to another without a second thought?

She'd assumed it would be the same for her but what had happened between her and Felipe that night transcended way beyond sex.

Her head was so full that it took a long time to fall back to sleep. When she finally did, there were no dreams.

CHAPTER ELEVEN

IN THE MORNING, Francesca awoke to find the bed empty and the sound of the shower running.

She looked at her watch. Seven o'clock.

The longest night of her life had passed very quickly.

When Felipe emerged from the bathroom, fully dressed in a navy suit and tie—she had no idea how he kept his suits so pristine—the strangest shyness passed over her.

'How are you feeling?' he asked, casting her that piercing, scrutinising gaze that made her belly flip.

'Like I could sleep the whole day.'

He smiled wryly. 'You can sleep on the plane. We're running late so you'll have to eat breakfast on the plane too. I don't want to rush you but we need to be at the airport within the hour.'

'I'll get a move on then.' Scooting out of bed, she brushed past him and locked herself in the bathroom.

She looked in the mirror, expecting to see a different face reflecting back.

She felt different. She felt as if her world had changed.

Everything that had passed in the night felt like a dream, her nightmare a dream within it.

Felipe had caught her at her lowest moment and carried her through it.

He'd listened without judgement. He'd held her. He'd comforted her.

And then he'd shared the darkest part of himself with her. He'd trusted her with that.

She couldn't begin to describe what that meant. All she knew was that it meant everything…

Her heart thumped erratically against her chest.

Oh, Dio, Dio, Dio.

This wasn't good. This was bad. Very bad.

She rubbed shampoo into her hair vigorously, scratching her nails into her skull.

She *couldn't* be falling for him. It wasn't possible. She'd only known him for five days.

That settled her.

Breathing a little more easily, she squeezed conditioner onto her palm and spread it through her hair.

This was her grief talking. Felipe had said so many times that her grief made her vulnerable and now she got what he'd meant.

A bad case of lust mixed with his tenderness and shared secrets were clouding her feelings. If she'd met him in different circumstances she was quite sure she'd still want him but her feelings wouldn't be so extreme. She wouldn't feel that she was standing on the edge of a precipice, waiting to fall into terrifying unknown depths.

Her grief, the situation they were in…it had all converged together to make her feel things that weren't true.

She wasn't falling for him.

She was still telling herself that when she hurried from the bathroom to her dressing room.

She was still telling herself that when she was fully dressed, had packed her stuff into her case and joined him in the suite.

And she was still telling herself that when he flashed her the smile that made her stomach melt into liquid butter.

'My men are all in position,' he told her.

It was time to go.

* * *

Francesca stared at the sleek white jet waiting on the runway in the distance. 'I thought we were going back on Pieta's plane.'

'It couldn't get to us until the afternoon so I had one of my own flown over.'

'I've always wanted to travel by private jet and now I get to go on two different ones in the space of a week? I'm being spoiled.'

'You didn't travel on the family jet when you were growing up?'

'What family jet?' she snorted. 'There was lots of family money, enough for us to be privately educated and see a lot of the world, but the *castello* needs a fortune to maintain it…'

'Your family has a castle?' he asked with surprise.

'It's in the middle of the family estate. I thought you knew that?'

'Pieta never spoke of it.'

'I don't think he liked it much. We used to spend summer holidays there but we never lived in it. Mamma found it too draughty. It's currently hired out for corporate functions and to ghost hunters.'

'Ghost hunters?'

'It's supposed to be haunted.'

'Did you ever find a ghost?'

'No, and I looked *everywhere.*'

He laughed.

'Daniele hid behind a gravestone in the cemetery once and jumped out on me, pretending to be a ghost, when I was about eight.'

'He would have been eighteen?'

'Yes. He was very mature for his age.'

He laughed even louder and shook his head. 'Your family has its own cemetery? That's quite an unusual thing to have, isn't it?'

'And a chapel. Until fifty years ago it had its own priest too. All the family on my father's side are buried there dating back to around the fifteenth century.' She attempted a smile even though her humour had drifted away from her. 'We buried Pieta next to my father. I suppose Daniele and I will end up there one day too.'

'It's a very different world from what I grew up with,' Felipe said, thinking of the plot in the packed cemetery in the middle of Alicante he'd paid for his father to be buried in. 'I can trace my lineage back only four generations.'

'Have you looked into it?' she asked, eyes lighting with curiosity.

'My mother did last year. There was nothing exciting to be found so she gave up.'

'There's always something exciting to be found in the past,' she insisted, 'but it's when people live in the past that there become problems. We have to respect the past but look to the future or everything stagnates.'

'Speaks the voice of experience?'

She pulled a face. 'If generations of my family had thought to maintain the *castello* rather than close rooms off when they became uninhabitable, it wouldn't be in the state it's in now.' Then she shrugged and gave an evil grin. 'Still, if Natasha isn't pregnant it'll be Daniele's problem now. Let him deal with it.'

'Didn't Pieta do anything to it?'

'He got builders and local craftsmen in to repair one wing, which is the part that's hired out, but…' She sighed. 'He never had the chance to follow it through.'

The car had come to a stop beside the plane, which was ready for boarding.

When they entered the cabin she stopped to take it all in, then nodded her approval. 'It's beautiful.'

This, his favourite of his planes, was the closest

Felipe had to a home, with a bedroom and fully functioning bathroom, dining and study area. He'd long ago decided that as he spent so much time travelling from one country to the next, he might as well do it in comfort and style.

They took their seats either side of a mahogany table and five minutes later they were airborne.

'I've just thought—aren't James and Seb coming with us?' Francesca peered out of the window as if she expected to see them flying up with jet-packs on to join them.

'They're staying in Aguadilla with my other men to prepare for our return on Saturday.'

'What preparations are needed?'

'Only the small matter of making sure we get you and four hundred thousand dollars of cash on and off Caballeros without you being kidnapped or the money stolen.'

'Oh. That.'

Oh. That. As if her safety meant nothing to her when it meant everything to him.

'Aren't you going to ask about any of the details?'

She raised her shoulders with utter nonchalance but her tired eyes were steady. 'Felipe, I am one hundred percent certain you will have every eventuality covered. I don't need the details. You just tell me what to do and when, and I'll do it.'

Something warm flowed into his veins at this and expanded, his blood flowing thickly into his every crevice.

People put their lives in his hands every day of the week but Francesca's utter faith in him meant more to him than all those people's trust combined.

He'd put his life on the line more times than he could ever count in the past eighteen years, had accepted it from the outset as a part of his job. But for the first time he knew he would gladly, not just willingly, lay down his life if meant keeping someone from harm. Her. Francesca. He would have his legs riddled with bullets if it stopped her being hurt.

And then the dreamiest of smiles crept over her cheeks. 'You can always fill me in on anything important while you're protecting me in Pisa.'

'Protecting you in Pisa?' he asked, raising his brow.

'Of course. What if those men who have been following me decide to fly out to Italy and hunt me down? You wouldn't leave me to that fate, would you?'

Even Felipe, who saw danger in everything, had to laugh at the absurdity of the notion, even as his blood thickened to treacle.

He'd planned to fly on to his headquarters in London after refuelling in Pisa.

But…

Did he really want to give up the chance to spend some proper time with this captivating woman, away from the dangers of Caballeros?

He no longer cared that he'd broken his rules and given in to his desire for her. He was beyond that.

He'd awoken with Francesca's leg draped over his thigh, her warm body pressed against him, and a powerful erection. He'd had to drag himself out of bed when all he'd wanted was to roll her onto her back and make love to her again, this time properly and with the tenderness that had been missing from their almost angry coupling before he'd discovered the truth that she'd been a virgin.

But getting her home to safety was his priority. Making love—if he was to make love to her again—would have to wait until they had the time and leisure to make it everything her first time should have been.

They'd shared with each other intimacies that went beyond their bodies. That in itself should have been enough to stop him making love to her again too.

In his younger years he'd had thoughts of settling down once his army days were done with but since Sergio's death and his own discharge the only life he could contemplate was one spent alone. He'd learned to fend for himself in his childhood and be content in his solitude. For Felipe, it was the natural way to be. Those long dark days spent fighting his injury to be able to walk again had made him see that.

But Francesca wasn't looking for anything heavy either. Neither of them wanted a proper relationship and he'd already broken all his rules with her…

In Pisa she wouldn't be under his protection. It would be just them, two consenting adults enjoying each other in a brief window of their lives.

For all his rationalising, it came down to one simple fact. He didn't want last night to be their only night.

'I can show you round the *castello*, if you like?'

she added temptingly, hitching her knees to snuggle more deeply into her seat.

'Now there's an offer I can't refuse.'

'And, of course, I'll make sure to obey your every command.'

'My *every* command?'

She covered her mouth and yawned widely. Her sparkling eyes were getting heavier by the second.

Dios, she was beautiful even with dark circles under her eyes.

The throbbing ache in his groin had him tempted to carry her straight into his bedroom but the moment was interrupted by a member of the cabin crew entering the cabin with the tray of coffee he'd asked for when boarding.

By the time she'd bustled out again, Francesca was fast asleep.

Francesca's heart pounded as she led Felipe into the elevator that went to her apartment floor.

He'd insisted on carrying her cases along with his own kit bag.

She still couldn't believe she'd found the nerve to invite him to stay with her. It had been the look in his eyes, the desire and tenderness she'd seen there as the jet had lifted through the clouds that had given her the courage.

They both knew it was only until their return to Caballeros. It didn't need to be vocalised. Neither wanted anything heavy or permanent.

But now that they were here, she found her nerves shredding her.

She'd never invited a man into her home before who wasn't related by blood.

Unlocking the front door, she took a deep breath. 'Coffee?'

He was staring around the apartment with evident interest. 'That would be good, thanks.'

She led him through to the kitchen, whispering a prayer of thanks to herself that the place wasn't a complete mess.

'I'm afraid I haven't got any milk.'

'Black's fine.'

'Give me a minute to call my mamma and let her know I'm back.' Fortunately, her mother's phone was switched off so she left a message to let her know she was home safely.

She put her phone on the kitchen island and swallowed. Felipe's presence in the large space seemed to have shrunk its proportions.

'This is a nice place,' he said, nodding approvingly. 'Much bigger than it looks from the outside.'

'Thank you.' She poured water into the pot and tried to control the tremble of her hands. Her movements felt awkward and stilted, as if she'd forgotten how to use her limbs. 'I can't take any credit for it—it belongs to Daniele. I just rent it off him. At a discount rate,' she added with the flash of a grin.

'What happened to your independence?' he teased.

'I'm independent, not stupid.' She strove to keep her tone light but it was so hard when she was massively aware that she was alone with Felipe in her apartment. Excitement thrummed through every part of her but the nerves were thrumming along with it. 'Daniele's got lots of properties. If he wants to rent one out cheaply to his little sister while she completes her education then his sister would be an idiot to say no. I moved in when I started university.'

'You did your law degree here in Pisa?'

She nodded and opened the fridge. 'Oh. I forgot. I haven't got any milk… I already told you that, didn't I?' She felt her cheeks burn to know she sounded like a bumbling idiot.

He stepped over and closed the fridge for her then trapped her against it, his large warm hands curving around her hips, his fingers biting into her flesh, his spicy scent sending her senses buzzing.

'Relax, *querida*,' he murmured, staring down at her. 'I'm not going to bite you.'

And then his lips came down on hers and she was swept into a kiss of such intoxicating hunger that she felt utterly dizzy when he finally let her go.

'Better?' he asked with a gleam.

'No,' she answered boldly.

With a sound that was a cross between a laugh and a groan Felipe dipped his head and kissed her again.

Her answering sigh loosened the tightness that had been coiled in his chest since he'd awoken. When she sank into him and kissed him back with the passion that was pure Francesca, a feeling he'd never known filled his heart to replace it.

How could he have ever thought himself capable of resisting her?

Francesca Pellegrini was a woman like no other, an intoxicating combination of strength and vulnerability he would lay down his life to protect.

Breaking the kiss, he took her face in his hands to gaze at her.

Light brown eyes shone back at him, then she took his hands from her cheeks and, holding them tightly, stepped backwards, taking him with her, her gaze not leaving his as she guided him back into the living room and through to her bedroom.

The shutters were closed, sunlight shining through a few of the slats to bring some relief to the duskiness, but he took no notice of anything else as she led him to large bed abounding with soft pillows and lay back on it.

So quickly he had no memory of his feet moving, he was on top of her, pinning her down with his hands holding hers tightly either side of her face, drinking in the beauty of what lay beneath him.

And then he kissed her. Slowly. Deeply. Relishing the softness of her lips. Breathing in the sweetness of her taste and her jasmine perfume.

When he pulled away to stare again she smiled and placed a hand on his cheek, rubbing the palm over the bristles of his beard, then raised her head to kiss him.

Her hands moved from his face to his neck and to the collar of his shirt. Her fingers played with the buttons with such clumsiness he couldn't believe he hadn't noticed her lack of experience that first time.

He put his hands to her waist and raised her up so they were both propped up facing the other.

Not a word was said.

Not a word needed to be said. Everything she wanted to say was right there in her eyes and from the expression in them she was reading his as well as he read hers.

Taking her hand, he placed it to his chest and held it there.

Had his heart ever beat as strongly?

Eyes now screwed with concentration she tentatively, but with growing confidence, unbuttoned his shirt until it fell open and he could shrug it off.

Now her eyes dilated and she pressed a kiss to the base of his neck and rubbed her cheek against his skin. Her gentle hands moved slowly across his chest, exploring him. He closed his eyes at the sensation of her touch firing through his veins.

His breathing became ragged as her fingers

drifted down to his abdomen and rested on the band of his trousers.

She marked his shoulder with the gentlest of kisses while she found the button to his trousers and popped it open after only the smallest of fumbles.

Last night he'd taken her in a madness of rage-filled lust. Now his desire burned as strongly as it had then but there was nothing else to compromise the thrills burning through him. Now it was just the two of them and the attraction that had been there from the very first look.

He stretched up higher so she could unzip him without constriction and with heightened colour blazing across her cheeks she pulled the zipper down. Then she swallowed before pinching the edges of his trousers and pulling them down to his thighs, taking his underwear with it.

Her eyes widened as his arousal sprang free.

'Can I touch it?' she asked tentatively.

He'd never had a woman look at him—all of him—with such unabashed desire. But there was shyness too and the whole mixture was intoxicating.

He brushed his hands through her hair as he'd

spent what felt like for ever dreaming of. 'You can touch and do whatever you like to me.'

Francesca was certain he must be able to hear her heart beating. It echoed through her ears, a rhythmic thrum that was almost painful.

Everything felt so different this time round.

Yesterday, she'd been too full of hurt and fury to care about being naked in front of him.

This time round she felt very much the virgin she had been.

She could hardly believe he was here and that this was happening.

Taking a breath, she raised herself to kneel too and lifted her dress over her head. Throwing it onto the floor, she then removed her bra and, with hands that now trembled wildly, tugged her panties down.

She was glad she'd forgotten to open her shutters before she'd last left her apartment. She could see him clearly and he could see her too but there was a haze that softened it. Romanticised it.

She swallowed her fear and forced herself to meet his eyes.

The desire pulsating from his stare was a look she knew she would remember for the rest of her life.

He shifted to remove his trousers and underwear, then knelt back so they faced each other, the tips of her breasts jutting against the hairs of his chest sending further tingles racing through her.

She put her hands to his chest as she'd done before and explored him with her fingers then followed that exploration with her mouth. His skin was smoother than she remembered from the night before and as she tasted and breathed in his muskiness she could feel her excitement building.

She heard the intake of air as she took his erection into her hand. It too was smoother than she'd expected but every bit as hard. It throbbed at her touch.

When they'd both lost their heads the night before, everything had been so urgent and immediate she'd not seen his erection before he was inside her.

Like the rest of him, it was magnificent, not at all ugly as she'd always imagined the male member to be.

His hands wove into her hair again but he made no further gesture of encouragement or expectation, letting her take things at her own pace, letting her go as far as she wanted, as far as she dared.

Dipping her head, she pressed her lips to the tip.

His groan was the encouragement she needed and she opened her mouth and covered the head.

And then he pulled away from her before she could take it any further.

'I'm sorry,' he said hoarsely, cupping her face in his hands. 'That feels too good. I don't want to come yet.'

The thought sent more pulses through her. He must have read her thoughts for he covered her lips with his.

'You can do it another time, *querida*, when I have more control over myself,' he murmured heavily into her mouth. 'But this time is for you.'

It thrilled her more than anything to know she had the power to make Felipe lose his control.

It thrilled her more to think of all the other moments they would share.

She wasn't after anything heavy or permanent, she reminded herself, knowing she *needed* to remind herself of this.

She wasn't in love with him, she was in lust. And if she felt as if she were under some kind of enchantment where all she could see and hear was Felipe then…

And then he laid her back down and kissed her so passionately that she stopped thinking at all.

Slowly, reverently, he made love to her.

There wasn't a part of her body left untouched or without the mark of his lips or the trail of his tongue. Every caress melted her a little more and soon she was nothing but a helpless mass of burning, sensual nerves.

He seemed to know exactly what she wanted and needed, rough and biting in places, tender and gentle in others, between her thighs and *there*, right in the very centre of her pleasure, coaxing her with his tongue until the explosion she'd felt at his hand on their drunken night happened again but this time deeper, longer, *more*…

When he snaked his way back up to kiss her deeply on the mouth, her head was spinning, her heart racing, the world around her gone to be just her and Felipe and her overwhelming need for his possession.

This time when he slid inside her she was more than ready for him.

The feel of him there, filling her, *completing* her…

And then he began to move and she lost what little of herself she'd had left.

It was too much. Overwhelming.

There was nothing she could do to stop it, to stop herself riding the waves, Felipe with her, and before she knew what was happening she was no longer riding it but soaring high off it into a world that dazzled her with the brilliance of its colour and the brightness of its stars, a world made purely of pleasure.

She didn't know how long she spent there. The journey back to earth was gentle, like a feather falling slowly through the breeze.

When she landed and opened her eyes, Felipe lay deliciously heavy on her, his breath hot on her neck.

After a long, long time he shifted his weight and moved his head onto the pillow beside hers and gazed at her with the same dazed look she knew must be in her eyes.

And then his gorgeous face widened into a grin and he laughed, though there was a shaky timbre to it. 'That was…'

'Better?' she supplied in the same shaky voice.

'No. It was incredible.' The grin faded. 'I didn't hurt you, did I?'

She palmed his cheek and slid a thigh between his. She'd never imagined it was possible to feel such closeness to someone. To feel as if she'd been one with them. 'The only way you can hurt me now is if we never do that again.'

CHAPTER TWELVE

THEY SPENT THE rest of the day in bed. By the time night fell, hunger of the more traditional kind took its hold and they ordered takeout. Francesca found a bottle of wine and they consumed it all it in her bed.

She was quite certain she'd fallen into a dream. None of it felt real and yet the intensity of her emotions were incredibly vivid.

She didn't want to probe what it all meant. All she wanted was to enjoy it for as long as it lasted before she returned to her real life.

Night turned into morning and she woke to crumpled sheets and an empty bed.

Immediate panic clutched her throat and she jumped out of bed at the same moment Felipe entered her room carrying two take-away cups and a fat brown paper bag.

'I couldn't find any food in your kitchen so I've brought breakfast,' he said with a grin, handing her one of the cups. 'This is a nice neighbourhood you live in. I always thought Pisa was nothing but its famous tower but it's surprised me.'

She took in the faded jeans and black T-shirt with the album cover of a punk band printed on it.

She hadn't seen him in jeans before and had had no idea he liked punk music.

'I also bring news—those men who were following you have been caught.'

'Have they? When? How?'

'I have a lot of contacts. One of them runs the foreign department for a country that will remain nameless. They in turn contacted Caballeros' president and made certain threats about foreign aid budgets. I got confirmation an hour ago that the men have been taken into custody. One of them was an employee in the Governor's house, the other two his cousins. The Governor has been warned that if anything untoward happens to you on Saturday night then he might find himself kicked out of office.' He gave a wry smile. 'Unfortunately corruption is everywhere. I have a feeling that the President will be sharing the bribe.'

'Threats, blackmail, bribery and corruption,' she said in awe. 'So that's how to run a country.'

He laughed but his eyes were serious. 'It happens to degrees everywhere but Caballeros is more extreme than others. Don't think it means Saturday will be plain sailing. We're still going to take every precaution.'

'I know you will.' From Felipe she expected nothing less. The threat those men had posed hadn't scared her as much as they should have simply because she'd known he would do everything in his power to keep her safe.

'Does this mean you don't have to stay and protect me any more?' she asked with a flutter of her lashes, although her heart was skipping all over the place in panic.

His eyes blazed as he opened the paper bag and offered first pick of the contents to her. 'It wouldn't do to take chances, would it?'

'Definitely not.'

'And you did promise me a tour of the *castello*.'

'I did.' She nodded solemnly. 'I'd be much safer there so maybe we should stay at the *castello* until we have to go back.'

'You're not afraid of the ghosts?'

Placing a hand to his chest, she pressed her lips to his neck. 'With you there to protect me, the ghosts wouldn't dare haunt us.'

* * *

Later that morning, they set off to the *castello* in a shining sports car Felipe had had delivered to them. Francesca had spoken to her mother, thinking she would drop in to check on her on the way, but had been relieved to hear she'd gone out for the day with her sister, Francesca's Aunt Rachele. It would have been hard explaining what she was doing with Felipe and she could hardly ask him to wait in the car.

Her mother was one of the strongest, most stoical people she knew. She'd nursed her husband through years of ill health and had buried her eldest child whilst making sure her roots were touched up first, but for the first time ever Francesca heard her mother's voice and thought how old she sounded.

Her poor mamma was suffering.

Thank God her mamma's younger sister lived with her. The two women rattled around the rambling villa on the Pisa Hills, driving each other slightly mad, but both would be lost without the other. It helped to know her mother had Rachele there.

Francesca hadn't mentioned she would be taking a guest to the *castello*.

Although she had no right of inheritance to the estate, tradition had always dictated that immediate members of the family had their own rooms and could have full use of the *castello*. Pieta hadn't changed that and she had her own key to the family wing.

Located on the Tuscan hills twenty short miles away from Pisa, Francesca felt the familiar curls of excitement in her belly when she caught her first glimpse of it, and couldn't resist staring at Felipe to watch his reaction.

He turned to her for a moment with a raised brow. 'Now, that is what you call a castle.'

She laughed. 'Wait until we get closer. You'll see how dilapidated it is.'

Encircled by a high wall Felipe estimated to be at least twenty feet high that had sentry towers at each corner, the castle dominated the countryside. Geometrically perfect, he couldn't begin to count the number of arched windows.

As they got closer, he began to see what Francesca meant about generations of Pellegrinis letting it fall into disrepair. Closer inspection revealed a crumbling fascia; what would once have been vibrant stonework faded into blandness.

He drove them into a courtyard where only

three other cars were parked. At the furthest point his eye could see, scaffolding had been erected. He guessed this was the latest part of the renovations Pieta had embarked on.

'Where are all the builders?'

'The renovations have been halted for a couple of weeks out of respect,' she explained with a sad shrug. 'There's staff here, I've let them know to expect us.'

'Does your family know you've brought me here?'

'No. They only come here to visit the cemetery. Papa and I were the only ones who liked staying here.' Her gaze cast off into the distance. 'Do you mind if I go to the cemetery?'

'Of course not. I'll come with you if you like.'

Leaving their stuff in the car, they set off to the salmon pink chapel that, unlike the rest of the castle, was in wonderful repair, proving Francesca's assertion of a family rooted in the past. She'd been the first to break free of the expectations built over generations. He admired her more than he could say.

The cemetery itself was chillingly beautiful, row upon row of highly glossed tombs and gravestones, all lovingly tended.

They stood in silence, hands clasped and heads bowed at the spot where Pieta lay buried next to his father. Vases of flowers sat in abundance.

What must it be like, he wondered, to be a part of a family that loved each other so dearly and protected each other almost mercilessly? And it didn't just extend to their bloodline. Natasha, Pieta's widow, was as much a Pellegrini as if she'd been born one. From everything Francesca had said, she'd been embraced into being a part of them.

For the first time he thought of his father with regret rather than indifference. He'd been someone who'd flitted in and out of their lives. Standing here now, he felt the loss of what his childhood could have been and wished that he could grieve for him the way a father should be grieved for.

He thought of his mother, now living a life of comfort and luxury but as remote in his adult life as she'd been in his childhood. He admired her enormously, knew the admiration was mutual. But how could they forge a true relationship when the foundations had never been properly built?

And then he thought of Sergio, who he'd mourned as if he'd lost a true brother.

'Shall we go to the *castello* now?' Francesca asked, her sombre voice cutting through his private reverie.

He pulled his lips in and nodded.

Being with Francesca felt different from anything he'd known before. Their time together was limited. He wanted to make the most of it before they said goodbye for good.

The family rooms were in the south of the *castello*, where renovation work had yet to begin. Francesca led him down a wide corridor that was so dark it brought to mind the horror films he'd watched on occasion as an unsupervised child. He could quite see why tales of it being haunted had been so believable to the impressionable Pellegrini children.

Francesca's room was something else.

'You slept in here as a child?' he asked with amazement.

'Yes. Not exactly child-friendly, is it? I loved it, though. I used to feel like a princess sleeping in this room.'

'Aren't the Pellegrinis descended from royalty?'

She shrugged. 'We haven't used the titles for generations. It's silly. How can you call yourself a prince or a duke if the title isn't recognised as meaning anything any more?'

Amply proportioned, the room had what would once have been vibrant gold and green wallpaper lining the walls but, like the *castello*'s fascia, it had faded into blandness. The ceiling, like the surrounding corridors, was of dark wood panels, laced with gold leaf. The same wood had been used to carve the enormous four-poster bed and headboard, and all the furnishings. Deep red velvet curtains hung on the tall windows, matching the inviting bedspread.

'If I ever get around to buying a home, I'd be tempted to have a bedroom like this.'

'Buy your own *castello*; you can afford it.'

'It would have to be warmer than this.' The early autumn sunshine that blazed down so brightly outside hadn't penetrated the thick stone walls. Given the choice, Felipe liked to be outdoors in the sun. He didn't like to think how cold the *castello* would be in the depths of winter.

'I told you it was draughty.' Throwing herself onto the bed, she rolled onto her belly and rested her chin on her hands. ‘Shall I call a member of staff and get them to light the fire?’

‘If you’re cold I’ve got a much better method of warming you.’

Her eyes gleamed. ‘I am *freezing*.’

And with that he proceeded to warm her more effectively than a dozen blazing fires.

Their time in the *castello* passed far more quickly than Francesca wanted. The live-in chef, thrilled to have something to do, produced delicious meals for them and in between eating and making love they explored the *castello* and its grounds. The only areas other than the chapel that had been maintained through the generations were the busy vineyards and cellar.

Felipe also had to spend time preparing for their return to Caballeros, liaising with his staff, approving plans…she didn’t want to know the details. She would leave that to the professionals. Leave it to him. She had no concerns about that at all. Indeed, it was kind of wonderful not having any concerns. Except…

‘This all feels so strange,’ she said to him while they paddled in the lake on the Friday afternoon. The cool water sloshed around her ankles, making her wish they'd been here the month before when the water had been warm enough to swim in. The seasons were changing. The leaves on the trees were thinning. Soon they wouldn't be green but autumnal reds and browns and yellows.

And she was changing with it.

She had to keep reminding herself there was no future for her and Felipe. These few days were the most they could have. She had her future to think of, the future she'd fought so hard to get. She was so close to qualifying she could almost touch it.

But a thought kept pushing itself to the fore.

Why did a relationship have to compromise her career or her independence?

Hadn't she made that promise to herself to feel life and embrace all it had to offer?

What was to say that once she'd established her career and was ready to settle down she would meet a man for whom she felt a tenth of what she felt for Felipe?

She'd never imagined she could feel such closeness to someone, a closeness that stretched far beyond desire.

She hadn't even known him for a week but it felt as if he'd been a part of her life for ever.

'What does?'

Francesca forced her mind back to the conversation.

It didn't matter how deeply her feelings had developed or how her outlook on life had changed, nothing could come of it. It didn't matter how tenderly he treated her now, Felipe had given no indication that his own feelings or outlook had changed. For him, their time together in Pisa was a short, sweet interlude before he resumed his real life, and she would be wise to remember that.

'This…doing nothing. I feel like I should be studying case files or working on one of the boring draft proceedings Roberto gave me. I can't remember when I last went this long without studying *something*.'

'Who's Roberto?'

'The senior lawyer Pieta put me under.'

'And why is it boring?'

She pulled a face. 'It's corporate law.'

After a few moments, Felipe said quietly, 'You don't have to stay at Pieta's firm.'

She glanced up at him.

'You don't enjoy it there.' It wasn't a question.

'It doesn't matter if I enjoy it or not. I'm committed.' She found corporate law as dull as dirty dishwater.

'You committed to working at Pieta's firm because you wanted to get closer to him.'

'What, and now he's dead I should abandon that commitment?'

'Did he think you would stay with him once you passed your bar exam?'

'No. He knew human rights was my long-term goal.'

'Did he try and talk you out of joining his firm and encourage you to go to a firm that specialised in human rights?'

She thought about it. 'Not really. It doesn't matter where I do my traineeship.'

'So he knew you joined his firm for him?'

'We never spoke of it in such terms but, yes, I suppose he must have known.' She remembered Pieta's genuine delight when she'd asked to do her traineeship with him. She remembered her disappointment when he'd put her under the wing of another senior lawyer and his explanation that she would need consistency while she did her traineeship. With all the travelling he did for his foundation he couldn't provide that consistency for her but was glad to be her mentor.

'So if he knew you were there for him, do you think he would think less of you if you were to move on now he's no longer here?'

'I can't think of this right now. It feels too disloyal.'

'All I'm suggesting is you think about it. It wouldn't be disloyal. Pieta would understand, I am certain of it. He wouldn't want you to waste two years working somewhere that didn't fulfil you.'

'Do not presume to tell me what my brother would have thought,' she snapped. 'If I, his own sister, wasn't privy to his private thoughts then I'm as sure as hell you wouldn't have been either.'

'Don't be so defensive. I'm not presuming anything.' He wrapped an arm around her waist and pulled her close.

Francesca sighed and rested her head in the crook of his arm, her sudden burst of guilty anger soothed by his touch. She *mustn't* allow herself to get used to it. 'I'm sorry. I know it's something I need to think about. And I will. There's a lot for me to consider. I'll probably have to go to Rome to practise if I want to make a success of it so if I were to make the change now then it would be silly not to go to Rome for my traineeship too.'

'You don't like Rome?'

'I love Rome, but it's a four-hour drive. I'm not like you. I'm happy to go away for a week or two but I always like coming home. I've never lived away from my family before. I thought I had another two years to get used to the idea.'

'Get Daniele to buy you a jet. That will make the distance seem closer.'

She laughed. 'He probably would if I asked nicely. There's a lot to think about—finding a firm to take me on, finding a place to live and all the small things that come with it. I will do it, though, whether now or when I've qualified for the bar. I've not worked so hard all my life to let it go to waste.'

He tilted her chin up and kissed her. 'Let's go back to the *castello* and I'll help clear your mind so you can think properly.'

'And how do you intend to do that?'

His hand found her bottom and squeezed it. 'I'm sure I can think of a few ways.'

Felipe sat on the Gothic armchair, watching Francesca get ready for their last meal in the *castello*.

He'd never watched a woman dress before. And

the woman doing the dressing was determined to put on a show.

They'd showered together and then he'd donned his suit while she had sat at the dressing table with a towel around herself and blow dried her hair.

He'd watched her moisturise her face and then skilfully apply her make-up, which to his mind did nothing but enhance the natural beauty she'd been blessed with. Then came the jewellery, a gold choker with a black sapphire that rested at the base of her slender neck, and matching earrings.

And then she had dressed.

First went on the underwear, functional and black, nothing in the least erotic about them, but…the way she slid the panties up her legs and thighs…

Dios, it was enough to raise his blood pressure to alarming levels.

Then she'd stared at him with challenge in her eyes.

She'd bet him he wouldn't be able to keep his hands to himself until after their meal.

'You're playing dirty,' he said when she cupped

her breasts to make sure they were perfectly encased in her strapless bra.

She flashed a wicked smile and then turned her back to him, bending over seductively to straighten her high black shoes before sliding her feet into them.

He smothered a groan.

Finally, she took the black dress off the hanger and slowly stepped into it.

When she turned round to face him a smile played on her lips. 'So, Señor Lorenzi, are you ready to escort me to dinner?'

Felipe swallowed back the lump in his throat that was as hard as the ache straining between his legs.

She'd never looked more beautiful. Or sexy. Her dress just begged to be ripped off, and she knew it. Strapless, like her bra, her cleavage sitting like ripe peaches, it was diagonally slashed, one side falling to her knee, the other to the top of her thigh.

She had done all this for him.

He cleared his throat.

Never mind keeping his hands off her until after their meal, he had no idea how he was going to walk away from her permanently.

CHAPTER THIRTEEN

THEY ATE IN the *castello*'s armoury, seated at the end of a polished oak table that could comfortably seat fifty people. Serena, the woman who managed the *castello* and was delighted to have guests in, had turned the enormous room with its frescoed ceiling, checked flooring and walls lined with bronzes and weaponry into a romantic fool's dream.

The chef had surpassed himself too. They'd been served an appetiser of beef carpaccio, followed by an aubergine tortellini. Their main course had been an exquisitely cooked boneless duck thigh in a berry and red wine sauce. Now they were making their way through their coffee and amaretto *semi-freddo*.

Francesca was thrilled with it all. The food had been dreamy, the service discreet. A fitting finale, she thought, to what had been the best few days of her life.

Tomorrow they would return to Caballeros then

stay the night in their hotel in Aguadilla. On Sunday morning they would go their separate ways…

She didn't want to think of that. If she blanked it out she could pretend there wasn't a clock frantically counting down the seconds until they had to say goodbye.

She peppered Felipe with questions about the music he liked and the places he'd been, asked for stories of his childhood escapades, drinking in his answers, committing them to memory because all too soon that would be all she had left of him. In return she regaled him with tales of summer holidays here in the *castello* and its long notorious history.

'How did you find the time to learn so much about it when you were always studying so hard?' he asked admiringly. He took the last bite of his *semi-freddo*, placed his spoon on the plate and pushed it to one side.

'Papa knew far more than me. He would tell me bedtime stories about the *castello* and our ancestors—some of them were *really* bloodthirsty.' She remembered the old tales with glee, not just the stories themselves but those happy times with her father. 'It was hard for him watching it fall into such disrepair but he was ill for a long time.

He spent as much of the income as he could on maintaining it but the priority was paying for full-time nursing care for him.' Her father had had motor neurone disease, which had gradually worsened through the years until in the months before he'd died he'd become immobile. It had been hard on all of them to see the strong man who had loved and raised them slowly disintegrate. Of all of them, she thought Daniele had suffered the most. She'd spent a lot of time with her father and when he'd died she'd had peace and acceptance as well as pain in her heart. Daniele's relationship with him had been difficult. He travelled even more than Pieta had and had rarely been there in those last few months. She didn't think he'd found either peace or acceptance.

'Was your father's illness the reason you chose to study in Pisa rather than further afield?' he asked, swirling Chianti in his wineglass.

'It was part of the reason but I think even if he hadn't been ill I would have stayed. I love my family. I wanted my independence but I wasn't ready to cut the apron strings completely. Moving into Daniele's apartment gave me the best of both worlds. It meant I could study and lead an independent life but be close enough that I could see my parents whenever I wanted and be there if they needed me.'

'And now?'

'And now I take stock and decide whether to make the move to Rome now or in two years.' She breathed deeply then admitted, 'I'm leaning towards doing it now. You were right earlier that Pieta wouldn't want me to spend the next two years unhappy and we both know life's too short. Mamma has Aunt Rachele living with her so she won't be alone.'

Felipe swirled his glass some more, nodding slowly. She recognised the expression. She'd learned to read all the expressions on his handsome face and knew this one meant he was thinking of something. She wished they had the time for her to learn everything about him.

'I can help you out with the living arrangements,' he said eventually.

'What do you mean?'

'Your surprise that I don't own my own home has got me thinking that it's time I invested my money. My life is always so busy I never think long term other than with the business and it's time to change that. I'll start by buying a house in Rome and when you're ready, you can move into it.'

His words were so unexpected that she gaped at him.

'Do I get a discount on the rent?' she asked cheekily when she'd regathered her wits. She must not read anything into his offer. She couldn't. Assumptions were dangerous.

That didn't stop her heart from setting off at a trot and for hope to start bashing at her chest.

'I wouldn't ask my lover to pay rent.'

She cleared her throat, the trot turning to a full-blown canter. 'Your lover? Does this mean…?'

His eyes holding hers steadily, he took a drink of his wine. 'I'm not ready to say goodbye. Are you?'

The ticking countdown in her head that had been beating like a drum in her ears suddenly exploded inside her, but instead of the misery she'd been dreading, unremitting joy burst through. All the dreams that had been building but which she'd shoved away from her mind, too scared to look at them, sprang free.

Her and Felipe. Together.

He wanted it too!

He didn't want to say goodbye either.

Was it possible, could it *be* possible, that he'd fallen in love with her as she had fallen in love with him…?

Love?

Oh, Dio, Dio, Dio.

Love?

Lightness filled her.

The truth had been staring her in the face for days.

Somehow, in this crazy week, she had fallen irrevocably in love with Felipe Lorenzi, and admitting it to herself was as heady and thrilling as it was terrifying.

She loved him.

Francesca swallowed, managing to produce a nod that could have been a shake of her head. 'I'm not ready to say goodbye either,' she said, her chest rising and falling so rapidly the words fought for release.

His eyes gleamed. 'Then a house in Rome is the perfect solution for us. An investment for me and a home for you.'

She loved the way *us* rolled off his tongue, how natural and right it sounded.

Us. Them. Together.

He drained his wine. 'Once I've bought it I'll

give you the money to decorate and furnish it to your tastes.'

Her mind immediately careered to the land of soft furnishings and huge carved beds. 'We can have a bedroom like my one here,' she said, thinking aloud, beaming her delight.

He refilled his glass and topped hers up with it. 'That will be up to you. You'll be the one living in it.'

She stared at him blankly, not understanding. 'Just me? What about you?'

'I never know from one week to the next where I'm going to be but I'll visit whenever I can.' Another gleam flashed in his eyes. 'I will be there to keep the bed warm when time allows, so make sure it's a big one.'

Visit?

When time allows?

The unfettered dreams that had been let off the leash came to a crashing halt.

'Right…' She nodded slowly, trying hard not to leap to conclusions, not to panic, to get straight the basic facts of what he was offering and what he wanted from her. 'So I'll be living in the house alone?'

He nodded. 'Mostly.'

'How often would we see each other? Weekly? Monthly?'

'You know I'm not in a position to answer that. You know the life I lead. If we weren't returning to Caballeros tomorrow I'd be back in the Middle East already. We'll see each other whenever I can.'

She swallowed before asking the question she most needed the answer to, trying to affect nonchalance. 'What kind of commitment will you want from me?'

His brows drew together before a wide smile broke over his face. 'We won't be in a relationship, *querida*. Don't worry, you'll still have your independence.'

His words were like a slap in the face.

That he seemed so pleased with himself only made it worse.

Sharp pain squeezed its way through at the crushing realisation she had got everything wrong.

She'd misread him entirely.

'It sounds like the kind of arrangement a man makes with his mistress,' she said slowly, trying to keep a hold of her wildly veering emotions, clamping on the nausea roiling violently in her belly.

'Mistress?' He made it sound as if he'd never heard of the word. 'A mistress is a woman kept by a married a man. I'm not married and I won't be keeping you. I'll have an investment, you'll have a home to live in and your independence, and we'll be able to see each other. It's the perfect solution.'

'No rent. No commitment. Sex whenever you fancy it. I'd be a woman kept for your convenience.'

He stared at her for too long. His dark eyes narrowed and glinted dangerously. 'That is not how it is.'

'That's what it sounds like.'

He'd made love to her like she meant something to him, he'd listened to her, he'd comforted her… and now all he wanted from her was sexual release when he could fit her in his schedule?

'You allow Daniele to help you. There is no difference.'

'There's *every* difference. He's my *brother*.' She pushed her chair back, the nausea growing. Bile had lodged in her throat. 'He charges me minimal rent because he loves me. He would let me have it for nothing.'

'I'm offering you a whole house for nothing.'

'No, not for nothing.' Now on her feet, legs shaking, Francesca jutted her chin in the air, no longer able to feign nonchalance. 'I thank you for your kind offer but I can't accept. I will not be your whore.'

And as she spoke, she looked down at what she was wearing and felt a wave of self-loathing.

She'd dressed like this to tantalise and torment him, had spent most of their meal imagining him peeling it off.

Wearing it like this now made her feel like a whore as much as his words did.

'My *whore*?' He shook his head as if clearing his ears of water, distaste etched on angry his face. 'How can you say such a thing? I thought you'd be pleased.'

Pulling the top of her dress up so it covered her cleavage and made it the respectable dress it should have been, she spat, 'Pleased to be your *concubine*? Pleased to be beholden to you, pleased to have you flit in and out of my life whenever it's convenient to you? How can I be pleased in a relationship that gives you all the power and when you won't even call it a relationship? Have you not learned anything about me?' She tugged the skirt of the dress down so the slash didn't ride so high.

Felipe was breathing heavily, staring at her with eyes that had turned to steel. Any tenderness that had been on his face earlier had been wiped away.

'You insult me,' he said, putting the palms of his hands on the tables and getting slowly to his feet. 'I have tried to help you. I have offered you more than I have ever offered anyone and you throw it back in my face.'

'I've insulted *you*?' she asked, outrage sweeping through her misery. 'You've just insulted everything we've shared together. You've cheapened it and you've cheapened me.'

'No, *you've* done that. I thought we understood each other but clearly I was wrong. I've offered you all I can. I will not be offering more. I live my life on *my* terms, *querida*. I've never lied to you. You know I don't have space in my life for anything permanent and you've told me enough times that you're not ready for anything permanent until you're established in your career. Or was that a lie?'

She tugged a weighty earring off her throbbing earlobe and threw it on the table, wishing she could throw it in his face. It hit her wineglass with such force it knocked it over, smashing it, the remnants of her wine spilling onto the oak.

She barely noticed.

'No, it wasn't a lie but my perspective's changed. I want to be happy and to feel life, and you make me feel *so much.*' She gazed at him, silently pleading for him to see the truth; that she loved him and that if he could only bring himself to give *something* of himself to her, something they could build on, something she could cling onto with hope in her heart, then her answer would be different. 'Having a relationship doesn't have to compromise my future, I see that now, but I still want a relationship of equals. What you're suggesting for us gives you all the power. I'd be at your mercy for the roof over my head. I can't be happy with a one-sided arrangement where the only commitment I'd get from you is that there will be no commitment. I want more than to be your concubine, Felipe. I want…'

But she couldn't continue. The words wouldn't come, not with Felipe's nostrils flaring as he breathed deeply, staring at her as if she were a stranger.

She'd heard many tones of voice from him but never had she heard such steely coldness as when he said, 'My offer is the most I'm prepared to give. Take it or leave it.'

The rip in her heart was so acute her knees almost buckled beneath her.

Somehow she managed to hold on, to keep herself upright, to eye him squarely. 'I choose to leave it.'

Total silence filled the room.

For a long time they did nothing but stare at each other.

Felipe was the one to break it. He nodded curtly. 'Then there is nothing left for us to say. I thank you for your hospitality. I will be in touch with instructions for tomorrow.'

Then he turned on his heel and strode out of the armoury, leaving her with nothing but the shattered remains of her wineglass and her head spinning at how quickly everything had disintegrated between them.

* * *

Francesca woke on her bedroom's sofa. The fire she'd lit had burnt to cinders, the room cold enough for her breath to mist.

Swinging her legs round, a pain shot through her neck. Great. She'd cricked it.

Her phone had fallen onto the floor. Holding a hand to her neck for support, she picked it up to check the time. Four o'clock in the morning.

She hadn't thought she would sleep. She'd curled up on the sofa unable to face getting in the bed that would have still been warm from their lovemaking, thinking she would wait it out until the sun came up.

Then she noticed a text message had come through.

She hesitated before swiping her thumb to open it.

A driver will collect you at your apartment at one p.m. to take you to the airport. Change into your dress before landing. You will be flown directly to Caballeros from Aguadilla.

It came from a number she didn't recognise but she didn't need to recognise it to know it came from Felipe. She'd shown him the dress she'd planned to wear to the Governor's party, anxious that he approved, not from a fashion point of view but from a safety aspect. Whatever promises had been made to him regarding her safety, the Governor's lecherous stares had given her the creeps. She wouldn't give him an inch of flesh to leer at.

She turned her phone off and staggered to the unmade bed.

She closed her eyes and swayed, the spinning in her head returning with a vengeance.

As she counted to ten, a pain, much like she imagined a punch in the stomach would feel, hit her, making her double over.

It took a long time to pass.

When she opened her eyes something black caught her eye, poking out from under her bed.

It was Felipe's black T-shirt with the punk band's album printed on it.

Felipe checked his messages.

Nothing new had come in since he'd last looked a minute ago. That was good.

All his men were in position. They'd run through the drill for all eventualities enough times that if anything should happen their reactions would be automatic.

He didn't expect anything to happen now. The Governor had called him personally to apologise for what the men had been planning and given his assurances that Francesca's safety and her entire project in Pieta's memory was guaranteed.

Felipe would not take anything for granted. The cash still needed to be handed over. Until that was done he knew he wouldn't be able to breathe easily.

A car appeared.

He checked his watch.

She was exactly on time.

James, who'd been waiting with Felipe by the Cessna, for once keeping his mouth shut, opened the back passenger door.

Francesca stepped out.

She'd shown him the dress she intended to wear. On the hanger, he'd thought it imminently suitable for the occasion, with its high rounded neck and long sleeves. Professional and elegant was the look she wanted to achieve, dressing for a party that was, for her, purely business.

She'd achieved it.

The black dress had delicate embroidered colours running the length of it and fell to her knees, lightly caressing her body. On her feet she wore electric blue high heels and carried a matching clutch bag. Her hair gleamed and hung loose like a waterfall.

His throat closed.

She looked stunning.

She met his eye. There was a moment of total stillness where not even the breeze stirred. He caught the briefest flash of emotion in her gaze before she inclined her head in greeting and walked the few paces towards him.

He turned and extended a hand to the open door of the Cessna, indicating for her to get in.

She obeyed the wordless gesture and climbed the stairs, her heels clanging on the metal steps, a cloud of her perfume trailing behind her.

Felipe gritted his teeth and followed her on board.

He had come close to bowing out of the whole operation and letting Seb take the lead on it. He'd got as close as calling Seb to tell him of the new plan but had found himself unable go through with it.

Despite the dark bitterness that curdled his insides at their angry parting, he could not bring himself to put her safety in someone else's hands.

The accusations she'd thrown at him…

He couldn't think of that now. He never wanted to think of it or think of her again.

When she was seated he showed her a tiny gold pin, no bigger than a centimetre in diameter.

'Wear this as a brooch. It has a tracking device in it.'

He dropped it into her open hand and watched her pin it securely.

James, who was sitting in front of them, watching his phone for the pin's signal, gave the thumbs up.

The Cessna rumbled down the runway and was soon in the air, flying high over the Caribbean Sea.

During the short journey from Aguadilla to Caballeros, he once again ran through the game plan with Seb and James.

Francesca didn't join in with the conversation.

If it wasn't for her perfume, filling the small cabin with its heady scent, filling him, he could tune her out entirely.

All he had to do was get this evening over with and then he could wash his hands of Francesca Pellegrini for ever.

CHAPTER FOURTEEN

TWINKLING FAIRY LIGHTS hung round the perimeter of the Governor's residence. Francesca looked at them, distaste rising through her as she thought of how half the island's electricity was still down almost three weeks on from the hurricane.

Her disgust grew when they entered the residence and discovered hundreds of people dressed to the nines. Squeals of laughter and raucous laughs echoed throughout. In the centre of the first room they were taken through to, was an enormous champagne fountain.

They found the Governor outside by his swimming pool wearing a white tuxedo, surrounded by a group of giggling women in bikinis young enough to be his granddaughters. The tall woman who'd first led her to him a week ago stood a short distance behind them, keeping guard, wearing a different white outfit than she'd worn then.

The Governor saw them and excused himself from his eager sycophants.

He greeted them like long-lost friends but with a wary eye at Felipe and asked about their journey, in English, polite talk that made Francesca think that whoever Felipe had got to put the screws on this man had tightened them like a vice.

She had to bite her cheek to prevent laughter escaping. She didn't doubt it would have a hysterical quality to it.

She *had* to keep her focus.

The Governor led them to his study, refusing even to let his all-in-white female shadow enter the room.

'Before we get down to business, a drink?'

He produced a bottle of brandy from the cabinet behind his desk.

'Why not?' she said before Felipe could say anything.

She might despise the Governor but she saw little point in antagonising him. The hospital still needed to be built and she would prefer his goodwill while it was being done.

He poured three hefty measures and handed them round. 'To new friends.'

Without meaning to, she caught Felipe's eye,

then quickly looked away and took too big a sip of the brandy.

It was easier to manage the entire situation if she kept him in the periphery of her vision rather than look at him directly.

She'd discovered that when she'd stepped out of the car at the airfield. She'd taken one look at him and had wanted to throw herself into his arms and beg him to never let her go.

She hadn't allowed herself to think of him since she'd got back to her apartment soon after the sun had come up, his T-shirt chucked in a bag which she'd intended to give back to him. Then she'd set to work. She'd stripped the bedsheets and boil-washed them, cleaned and polished, vacuumed every inch of flooring, all the while refusing to allow the nausea and dizziness that kept racking her to derail her from her mission.

Then she had packed her evening dress and some clean clothes to change into for the return flight home and waited to be collected.

She hadn't expected him to be the one to collect her but that hadn't stopped her belly dropping with disappointment when she'd opened the door to find Seb there.

She hadn't expected him to be on the plane

either but, again, unmistakable disappointment had punched her to find she would be making the flight with only Seb and the cabin crew for company.

By the time they landed in Aguadilla, with no sign of Felipe at the main airport, she'd convinced herself that he wouldn't be there at all, so to see him when they entered the airfield, standing in front of the Cessna, had hit her like another punch.

At least she'd had a minute to compose herself before having to get out of the car and face him looking so sickeningly handsome in a black tuxedo. He could wear anything and he would still be sexiest man in a thousand mile radius.

She didn't know what she'd expected to see in his eyes when she faced him. Acrimony? Disgust? But apart from one brief flash of emotion, which she could quite easily have imagined, there had been nothing there. His eyes were blank.

He'd reverted back to the authoritative, arrogant man she'd first met a whole lifetime of a week ago.

The brandy burned then numbed her throat. She welcomed it. If she drank the whole glass it might numb the rest of her twisting insides too.

'I wish to apologise for the behaviour of my staff member,' the Governor said, settling on his captain's chair. 'I was very shocked when I heard.'

I just bet you were.

'I have your assurance it won't happen again?' she asked pleasantly.

'You have my word.' He said it as if his word should mean something. Then his left eye twitched. 'You have the money?'

She glanced at Felipe without fully looking at him.

He placed the briefcase he'd been carrying since they left the Cessna on the desk. Only then did she notice the glint of metal around his wrist.

She'd been avoiding looking directly at him so effectively that she'd failed to see he'd handcuffed the briefcase to his wrist.

He pulled the key out of his pocket and unlocked the cuffs.

The briefcase sprang open. He twisted it around and pushed it to the Governor.

The older man flicked through the case, nodding his approval, then pulled open a drawer and removed a stack of papers. He handed them to Francesca.

'The deeds to the site. We both sign them.'

Tempted though she was to read them quickly, she made herself sit down and read it through properly.

Written in English, it was concise and unambiguous. When she put her name to it the site would belong to Pieta's foundation.

Thirty minutes after entering the Governor's study the job was complete.

Before they left his office, Felipe turned to him and fired off something in Spanish.

She didn't have a clue what he said but the Governor's face went as white as his teeth.

She had a feeling the hospital would be built without any problems whatsoever.

Felipe rode up front with James on the drive back to the airport, leaving Francesca in the back with Seb.

The stars twinkling in the black sky reminded her of a purer version of the Governor's fairy lights. Thank God she'd never have to see him again.

Soon she would never see Felipe again either. Her part in the project was over.

His jet waited on the runway exactly where they'd left it.

She would travel back to Pisa alone. Felipe and the others had another plane coming to collect them in the morning, taking them on to whatever dangerous part of the world they were working in next.

Fighting a closing throat, Francesca said, 'Thank you, gentlemen, for everything you've done for me.'

James turned his head to look at her.

'No worries,' he said. Was that sadness she saw in his grin? 'It's been fun.'

She gave a hollow laugh. 'I think that's enough of that kind of fun for me. Keep safe.'

With James and Seb's farewells echoing in her ears, she got out of the car.

Felipe, who hadn't exchanged a direct word with her since giving her the tracking pin, got out with her and shut the door behind him.

They stood by the car in a silence that grew tauter with every passing second.

He was close enough for her to raise her hand and touch him but the distance between them was greater than it had ever been.

She wished he'd never made his offer of a

house. She wished she'd never had that leap of joy when she'd misinterpreted the offer as one of a home for them both. She wished she was still ignorant of the extent of her feelings for him.

Felipe was a lone wolf without roots, roaming with his pack but apart, never breaching the distance he'd created with them. He would never settle down, not in one place and not with one person. His wounds from his past were too deep.

She was more of a homing pigeon. She needed her roots and her family.

Telling herself all this didn't stop the crushing weight in her chest at all that could have been and all that had been lost.

'I congratulate you on getting the deeds,' he said stiffly. His eyes rested in the distance over her shoulder. 'You did well.'

'Thank you,' she whispered. She put her fingers to her neck and to the pulse beating frantically in it. It felt like her heart was crying.

The door to the jet opened and one of the cabin crew put his put his head out. 'Control's been on the radio. We have ten minutes to get airborne.'

Now Felipe did meet her eye, and in that glance

she thought she saw a glimpse of all the misery and pain she felt inside herself.

And then he turned and got back in the car.

Felipe wouldn't allow James to drive away until the plane carrying Francesca was indistinguishable from the stars themselves.

'We can go now,' he said bleakly.

In silence, James pulled away.

Felipe rested his head against the window and closed his eyes. He could still feel her breath on his face.

His heart had never felt heavier.

Dios, he could still hear her laughter ringing in his ears, like an echo.

He had to stop this. She'd made her choice. What he had to offer and what she wanted were worlds apart.

'Are you okay, boss?' James asked. For once his tone was serious.

'Why wouldn't I be?'

'No reason. You look like you have something on your mind, that's all.'

'Well, I haven't.'

'Funny job we do, isn't it?' James said, ignoring the 'shut up' warning tone Felipe had just given him. 'Putting our bodies on the line every day for people we don't know and half the time don't even like, preparing to take a bullet for each other, but ask us to put our hearts on the line for someone special and we run away screaming like frightened schoolboys.'

'James?'

'Yes, boss?'

'Shut up.'

Two weeks later and Felipe could still hear James's words as fresh and as painful as when he'd first uttered them.

'Ask us to put our hearts on the line for someone special and we run away screaming like frightened schoolboys.'

Is that what he was doing? Running away?

He'd been upfront with Francesca from the start. She was the one who'd changed. He'd never lied about his feelings. He'd offered her an inch and she'd wanted a mile. She'd wanted more than he was capable of giving. Much more.

He'd seen it in her eyes, a hope for something he could never give her.

He wouldn't even be thinking of her if Daniele

hadn't just called him to discuss protection for his men during the hospital's construction.

They'd come to the end of the conversation before he'd asked the question that had played on his lips since he'd first heard Daniele's voice. 'How's Francesca? Keeping out of trouble?'

Daniele hadn't sounded surprised at the question. 'She's doing okay on the surface. Getting ready for her move to Rome…'

'Rome?'

'Didn't you know?' He'd sounded surprised that Felipe wasn't privy to all Francesca's private doings. 'She's transferring her traineeship to a firm there. She starts in January.'

A spark of pride had flickered in his numb chest. She was doing it.

Daniele continued speaking. 'But to be honest with you, I'm worried about her. I don't think she's sleeping and I'm sure she's not eating properly, which is not like her at all. I'm taking her out to lunch in an hour to try and get some food into her.'

'She's grieving,' Felipe had said automatically. 'You all are.'

'I hope that's all it is.'

And Felipe hoped that's all it was too.

At least Francesca had her family watching her, ready to catch her if she should fall too far.

He rubbed the back of his neck with both hands. *Dios*, he was tired. Like Francesca, he was having trouble sleeping.

He had no appetite either. All the food he'd consumed recently had been for the purposes of fuel.

He felt like he'd spent the past two weeks in a form of limbo, going through the motions of his life but with no real animation.

There was an emptiness inside him he'd never known before.

'I *am* eating,' Francesca hissed. She speared a gnocchi and popped it in her mouth, making a big deal of chewing and swallowing it. 'See?'

Daniele did not look impressed. 'Eat another one.'

She complied moodily. It was as tasteless as the first.

'I spoke to Felipe Lorenzi earlier,' he said casually.

Hearing the name spoken was as painful as climbing into her empty bed.

'That's nice,' she managed after a pause that went on long enough for Daniele's eyebrows to rise.

'He asked after you.'

'Did he?'

Oh, God, her pathetic heart was battering her ribs again.

'What happened between you two?'

'Nothing.' Her lie was automatic. She couldn't talk about Felipe to anyone. Somehow she knew that if she started to talk about it she would start to cry and if she started to cry there was a danger she would never stop. Desperate to divert his attention, she said, 'Have you received the hotel bill yet?'

Her diversion worked.

'What hotel bill?'

'From when I was in Aguadilla. I hope you scrutinised it. I made sure to have all the most expensive items off the menus.' It was a struggle to keep her voice light to the end of her sentence.

Aguadilla and Caballeros would always be bound in her mind with Felipe.

'I didn't pick up the tab,' he said, looking confused. 'I had nothing to do with it.'

'Then who…?'

But as she asked the question she realised she knew who'd paid.

'Daniele, did you pay the bribe?' She'd gone through the foundation's accounts. The site bill had been paid but there was no evidence of the bribe money leaving the accounts. Alberto had taken leave again and wasn't answering her calls so she hadn't been able to check with him where the money had come from.

'What bribe?' His face darkened. 'What have you done?'

'Nothing,' she said hastily. 'I nearly did but Felipe stopped me. He sorted it.'

And he hadn't told her family.

Felipe hadn't only saved her from killing her career before it had even started but had saved her from the humiliation of her family's disappointment in her.

He must have paid the bribe from his own money.

'Francesca, what's wrong?'

With a start she realised she was crying, tears pouring out of her so thickly her brother's face blurred before her.

She'd been right to fear them because now they'd started she couldn't stop them.

She'd lost him. Her big, strong, arrogant protector, who had done everything in his power to save her from herself, had comforted her, shouted at her, laughed with her and made love to her.

She'd lost him and there was nothing she could do about it. He would never love her.

He couldn't stop thinking about her.

The call with Daniele had made it worse.

Now he couldn't stop himself worrying that she was eating.

When he retired to bed that night in another opulent but generic hotel room, this one in Dubai, he closed his eyes and thought of her.

Was she thinking of him?

Could he be the reason she couldn't sleep? Or was that just the arrogance she'd often accused him of coming out? Or wishful thinking?

He pulled a faded photo from his wallet. Him and Sergio in their army gear, shades on, arms slung around each other's shoulders, wide grins on their faces.

Sergio had had an infectious zest for life. He'd thrown himself into every part of it, his enormous smile never far from his face. In that respect he'd been similar to Francesca, who never committed to anything half-heartedly. With Francesca it was all or nothing.

He sat up straighter and dug his fingers into his skull.

All these years he'd been on his own…

It suddenly dawned on him that if Sergio could see him now he would slap him round the head.

James had been right that they put their bodies on the line every day, for people they didn't know as well as for each other. It had been the same in army. They'd all known the risks from the moment they'd signed on. Sergio had known it, his other fallen comrades had known it.

Sergio's wife had moved on. She'd remarried and had another child. Sergio would have wanted that for her.

So what was stopping *him* from moving on too? Why had he retreated to the familiar childhood loneliness he'd joined the army to escape?

He'd kept to himself all these years because the loss of Sergio and the family he'd found in his army career had been so great it had been safer for him. No attachments meant he couldn't be hurt again. But how was this any safer, sitting in a room sick to his guts missing the only woman in the world who could make him laugh and drive him to fury in the space of one conversation?

When he'd made his offer of the house to her he'd believed he was offering the most he could give but now, twisting it round, he could see he hadn't offered her anything, not of himself.

He'd been alone for the greatest part of his life but only now, without Francesca in his life, did he truly feel lost.

If her brother didn't take his finger off the intercom Francesca was going to throw something at him.

Couldn't he take the hint? She didn't want to see him.

She'd cried in the restaurant for a good fifteen minutes. Luckily her back had been turned on most of the other diners so no one other than Daniele had seen the silent waterfall pouring down her cheeks. He'd wanted to take her to their mother's house but she'd dug her heels in and insisted he take her home.

She'd needed to be alone. She'd told him that. She'd thought he'd respected that.

Fine, he wanted to check on her, but at six

o'clock in the morning? So what if she hadn't been to sleep yet.

He wasn't giving up. He must have decided to just leave his finger on the buzzer until she gave in.

Throwing the bedcovers off, she stomped to the intercom. She picked up the receiver and yelled, 'Come in then!', pressed the button to admit him, and then flung her front door open.

She might as well make a coffee now that she was up. If Daniele was lucky, she might not throw it in his face.

But the man who entered her apartment wasn't her brother.

She stared from the kitchen door in disbelief, unable to speak, unable to move, unable to even breathe.

It was *him*. Felipe. There. *Here*. In her apartment.

Blood rushing to her head, she had to grind her bare toes into the floor stop herself from swaying or running to him, had to blink frantically to stop the tears that had welled in her eyes like a tap being turned on from falling.

He closed the door behind him and gazed at her with an expression she didn't recognise, his throat moving but no words coming from his mouth.

'Why are you here?' she whispered, breaking the silence.

His shoulders rose, a huge sigh escaping him. 'I'm sorry to turn up like this.'

'What's wrong?' He looked so haggard, something terrible must have happened.

'Nothing's wrong. No…' He cleared his throat. '*Everything's* wrong. I can't go on like this. I've been a fool. The biggest fool. I'm lost without you. I'm here to say sorry. I'm here to ask you… No, to *beg* you to forgive me.'

Her heart pounding, head spinning, Francesca stared in disbelief at the face she had missed with a desperation she hadn't thought possible.

'You were right. Everything you said. What I offered was an insult to everything we'd been together. I thought I was meant to be alone, I've spent so long telling myself that I had come to believe it as fact. I thought it was the way nature had made me but it wasn't. I was just protecting myself from being hurt again but you slipped into my heart without me realising and I can't bear to be without you a minute longer. I want to be with you. I know I don't deserve it but I am begging you, please, give me the chance to make things right. I love you, *querida*.'

His words filled her head with a dazed amazement.

He loved her?

Was she dreaming? Had the sleep that had been so impossible to find these past few weeks finally enveloped her and given her what she yearned for?

'Please, *querida…*' His voice broke. 'Say something. Shout at me. Hit me if you must. Whatever you need. I deserve it. If it's too late for us then tell me and I'll leave but if you can find it in yourself to forgive me I swear I will give all of myself to you. Whatever you decide, know that I will always be yours and my heart will always belong to you.'

She continued to stare, taking this all in, slowly starting to believe that this was really happening, and then her feet ungrounded themselves and her legs moved for her, towards him, running the steps needed to throw herself into his arms.

He caught her and held her tightly, close enough for her to feel the beating of his heart through the hardness of his chest and feel his breath in her hair, so solidly *real*, and she buried her face into the open collar of his neck and inhaled his scent and warmth.

She wasn't dreaming. He was here.

And he loved her.

Felipe closed his eyes tightly as he breathed her in and nuzzled into the soft cheek he had thought he would never feel again.

He hadn't known what reception he would receive and this…it was more than he had dared hope for.

Once he'd acknowledged to himself just how deeply his feelings for her ran, madness had taken its grip. All he could think was that he needed to get to her, no cares for the people he'd had to wake to get him there. He would have dragged a thousand people out of bed to get to her.

After the longest time he shifted so he could take her face in his hands and examine her closely. His heart lurched. Her beautiful face had a haunted quality to it, her eyes hollow with dark circles running under them. '*Querida*, are you ill?'

'I've been… I've not had an illness. I've…' A solitary tear fell down her cheek and she closed her eyes.

'Look at me, *querida*,' he commanded gently.

When she opened them he wiped another falling tear with his thumb before taking her hand and pressing it to his thundering heart.

'Do you feel that? It hasn't beaten the same since I met you. It's yours.'

'Oh, Felipe,' she whispered. 'I've been so unhappy without you. I go through the motions but I can't sleep. I'm struggling to concentrate. I have to make myself eat. I never knew what it meant to be heartsick but that's how it's been, like my heart's been broken.'

Something so strong filled him, threatening to burst out of his chest.

Her hand found his cheek and rubbed the bristles of his jaw lovingly then the widest, most beautiful smile lit her face. 'I love you, Felipe.'

Even though her feelings shone out of her eyes he still didn't dare believe it. 'You do?'

She nodded, her hand still stroking his face. 'I don't want to be without you and if you mean what you say and if there's a chance we can make it work then I want to take it because being here with you right now… I can breathe again.'

Hearing those words was like being handed a gift-wrapped box of happiness.

'Oh, my love,' he breathed, and finally allowed himself to kiss her. 'Marry me.'

'Marry you?'

'Marry me. No half-measures. I want everything with you. The full commitment. A marriage of equals. If you say no then I will accept that without—'

'Yes,' she interrupted.

'You don't want to think about it?'

'No.'

'No, what?'

'No, I don't want to think about it. I want to marry you.'

'Are you sure?' He searched anxiously into her eyes, which were bright again with tears. 'You look as if you're about to cry.'

'Yes! And I'm about to cry because you've just made me the happiest woman alive!'

'I have?'

'You have a lot to learn about women.' And with that she pulled his head down to smother his mouth and face with kisses.

It was only when he lifted her to carry her into the bedroom that he noticed what she was wearing.

'Is that my T-shirt?'

She beamed. ‘It *was* your T-shirt.’

‘You sleep in it?’

‘Every night. It was the only thing of yours I had left.’

That one thing convinced him more than anything else that Francesca Pellegrini loved him as much as he loved her.

He carried her to the bedroom, reflecting that he was the luckiest man who had ever lived.

EPILOGUE

TWO YEARS LATER, Francesca Lorenzi waddled through the front door of her beautiful house in Rome holding onto her huge belly and hoping her husband had beaten her home. She hadn't seen him for two days and had missed him dreadfully. With their first child due in four weeks, they were both clearing their desks—Felipe metaphorically—so they could spend some time together alone to prepare.

Instead of finding a quiet home, she walked in to find her entire family there, mother, mother-in-law, siblings, cousins, aunts, uncles and, of course, her husband standing there with an indulgent expression on his handsome face.

'Surprise!'

'I haven't had the baby yet,' she said, laughing, allowing herself to be engulfed in a wave of careful hugs and wet kisses.

'This is to celebrate you qualifying for the bar,' her mother explained.

'I tried to stop them,' Felipe said.

'Liar.'

'He is a liar, it was his idea,' Aunt Rachele said.

Felipe pulled her into an embrace and whispered, 'You've worked so hard for this. We all wanted to show you how proud we were.'

'I couldn't have done it without you,' she whispered back before kissing him.

He'd been her rock.

After that dream morning when he'd turned up at her apartment declaring his love for her, he'd set about putting into motion all the changes needed for them to be together properly. The first thing he'd done was hire a PA for himself. The second thing had been to promote Seb to Chief Executive of all operations.

He'd opened a base in Rome on the same street as the human rights law firm she'd joined, and restructured the way things were run so he could be home at night with her the vast majority of the time. Seb now ran all the operations with James as his deputy. The two men were here now, and she greeted them warmly while keeping a tight hold of her husband's hand. She always kept a tight hold of it.

Felipe sometimes felt he should pinch himself to make sure he hadn't slipped into a dream.

He'd never had any doubts that stepping back from the operational side of the business was the best thing for him and Francesca. He'd expected to miss the adrenaline and excitement that had come with it, but…nothing. He hadn't missed it at all. His passionate, open-hearted wife was all the excitement he needed.

Finally, he had the family he'd always craved but had stepped away from seeking. Her family had embraced him so deeply as one of their own that often he thought he should have been the one to take her surname rather than the other way round. Francesca had been the one to encourage him to get closer to his own mother, surprising him by inviting her to stay with them for a long weekend. Loving Francesca had given him a greater understanding of the love his mother had for him. She'd sacrificed everything for him, just as he would gladly sacrifice everything, his wealth, his business, his life, for Francesca. Slowly they were building towards a proper mother-son relationship and now he felt the love for her in his heart like a pulse. She adored her daughter-in-law.

As he led the toast to his wife and all her amazing accomplishments, he marvelled for the thousandth time that he was indeed the luckiest man to have ever walked the earth.

Two weeks later, Sergio Pieta Lorenzi was born, weighing seven pounds and one ounce.

Everyone said he had his father's looks and his mother's temper.

* * * * *

If you enjoyed the first part of Michelle Smart's
BOUND TO A BILLIONAIRE *trilogy*
look out for

CLAIMING HIS ONE-NIGHT BABY
Coming January 2018

BUYING HIS BRIDE OF CONVENIENCE
Coming February 2018

In the meantime why not explore another
Michelle Smart trilogy?

THE KALLIAKIS CROWN
TALOS CLAIMS HIS VIRGIN
THESEUS DISCOVERS HIS HEIR
HELIOS CROWNS HIS MISTRESS

Available now!

MILLS & BOON®

Large Print – December 2017

An Heir Made in the Marriage Bed
Anne Mather

The Prince's Stolen Virgin
Maisey Yates

Protecting His Defiant Innocent
Michelle Smart

Pregnant at Acosta's Demand
Maya Blake

The Secret He Must Claim
Chantelle Shaw

Carrying the Spaniard's Child
Jennie Lucas

A Ring for the Greek's Baby
Melanie Milburne

The Runaway Bride and the Billionaire
Kate Hardy

The Boss's Fake Fiancée
Susan Meier

The Millionaire's Redemption
Therese Beharrie

Captivated by the Enigmatic Tycoon
Bella Bucannon